THE COUNTRY
OF THE POINTED FIRS

by SARAH ORNE JEWETT

Martino Publishing
Mansfield Centre, CT
2015

Martino Publishing
P.O. Box 373,
Mansfield Centre, CT 06250 USA

ISBN 978-1-61427-833-7

© *2015 Martino Publishing*

Cover design by T. Matarazzo

Printed in the United States of America On 100% Acid-Free Paper

THE COUNTRY
OF THE POINTED FIRS

by SARAH ORNE JEWETT

BOSTON AND NEW YORK
HOUGHTON MIFFLIN COMPANY
The Riverside Press Cambridge

Contents

I

The Return

THERE WAS SOMETHING about the coast town of Dunnet which made it seem more attractive than other maritime villages of eastern Maine. Perhaps it was the simple fact of acquaintance with that neighborhood which made it so attaching, and gave such interest to the rocky shore and dark woods, and the few houses which seemed to be securely wedged and tree-nailed in among the ledges by the Landing. These houses made the most of their seaward view, and there was a gayety and determined floweriness in their bits of garden ground; the small-paned high windows in the peaks of their steep gables were like knowing eyes that watched the harbor and the far sea-line beyond, or looked northward all along the shore and its background of spruces and balsam firs. When one really knows a village like this and its surroundings, it is like becoming acquainted with a single person. The process of falling in love at first sight is as final as it is swift in such a case, but the growth of true friendship may be a lifelong affair.

After a first brief visit made two or three summers before in the course of a yachting cruise, a lover of Dunnet Landing returned to find the unchanged shores of the pointed firs, the same quaintness of the village with its elaborate conventionalities; all that mixture of remoteness, and childish certainty of being the centre of civilization of which her affectionate dreams had told. One evening in June, a single passenger landed upon the steamboat wharf. The tide was high, there was a fine crowd of spectators, and the younger portion of the company followed her with subdued excitement up the narrow street of the salt-aired, white-clapboarded little town.

II

Mrs. Todd

LATER, THERE WAS only one fault to find with this choice of a summer lodging-place, and that was its complete lack of seclusion. At first the tiny house of Mrs. Almira Todd, which stood with its end to the street, appeared to be retired and sheltered enough from the busy world, behind its bushy bit of a green garden, in which all the blooming things, two or three gay hollyhocks and some London-pride, were pushed back against the gray-shingled wall. It was a queer little garden and puzzling to a stranger, the few flowers being put at a disadvantage by so much greenery; but the discovery was soon made that Mrs. Todd was an ardent lover of herbs, both wild and tame, and the sea-breezes blew into the low end-window of the house laden with not only sweet-brier and sweet-mary, but balm and sage and borage and mint, wormwood and southernwood. If Mrs. Todd had occasion to step into the far corner of her herb plot, she trod heavily upon thyme, and made its fragrant presence known with all the rest. Being a very large person, her full skirts brushed and bent almost every slender stalk that her feet missed. You could always tell when she was stepping about there, even when you were half awake in the morning, and learned to know, in the course of a few weeks' experience, in exactly which corner of the garden she might be.

At one side of this herb plot were other growths of a rustic pharmacopoeia, great treasures and rarities among the commoner herbs. There were some strange and pungent odors that roused a dim sense and remembrance of something in the forgotten past. Some of these might once have belonged to sacred and mystic rites, and have had some occult knowledge handed with them down the centuries; but now they pertained only to humble compounds brewed at intervals with molasses or vinegar or spirits in a small caldron on Mrs. Todd's kitchen stove. They were dispensed to suffering neighbors, who usually came at night as if by stealth, bringing their own ancient-looking vials to be filled. One nostrum was called the Indian remedy, and its price was but fifteen cents; the whispered directions could be heard as customers passed the windows. With most remedies the purchaser was allowed to depart unadmonished from the kitchen, Mrs. Todd being a wise saver of steps; but with certain vials she gave cautions, standing in the doorway, and there were other doses which had to be accompanied on their healing way as far as the gate, while she muttered long chapters of directions, and kept up an air of secrecy and importance to the last. It may not have been only the common ails of humanity with which she tried to cope; it seemed sometimes as if love and hate and jealousy and adverse winds at sea might also find their proper remedies among the curious wild-looking plants in Mrs. Todd's garden.

The village doctor and this learned herbalist were upon the best of terms. The good man may have counted upon the unfavorable effect of certain potions which he should find his opportunity in counteracting; at any rate, he now and then stopped and exchanged greetings with Mrs. Todd over the picket fence. The conversation became at once professional after the briefest preliminaries, and he would stand twirling a sweet-scented sprig in his fingers, and make suggestive jokes, perhaps about her faith in a too persistent course of thoroughwort elixir, in which my landlady professed such firm belief as sometimes to endanger the life and usefulness of worthy neighbors.

To arrive at this quietest of seaside villages late in June, when the busy herb-gathering season was just beginning, was also to arrive in the early prime of Mrs. Todd's activity in the brewing of old-fashioned spruce beer. This cooling and refreshing drink had been brought to wonderful perfection through a long series of experiments; it had won immense local fame, and the supplies for its manufacture were always giving out and having to be replenished. For various reasons, the seclusion and uninterrupted days which had been looked forward to proved to be very rare in this otherwise delightful corner of the world. My hostess and I had made our shrewd business agreement on the basis of a simple cold luncheon at noon, and liberal restitution in the matter of hot suppers, to provide for which the lodger might sometimes be seen hurrying down the road, late in the day, with cunner line in hand. It was soon found that this arrangement made large allowance for Mrs. Todd's slow herb-gathering progresses through woods and pastures. The spruce-beer customers were pretty steady in hot weather, and there were many demands for different soothing syrups and elixirs with which the unwise curiosity of my early residence had made me acquainted. Knowing Mrs. Todd to be a widow, who had little beside this slender business and the income from one hungry lodger to maintain her, one's energies and even interest were quickly bestowed, until it became a matter of course that she should go afield every pleasant day, and that the lodger should answer all peremptory knocks at the side door.

In taking an occasional wisdom-giving stroll in Mrs. Todd's company, and in acting as business partner during her frequent absences, I found the July days fly fast, and it was not until I felt myself confronted with too great pride and pleasure in the display, one night, of two dollars and twenty-seven cents which I had taken in during the day, that I remembered a long piece of writing, sadly belated now, which I was bound to do. To have been patted kindly on the shoulder and called "darlin'," to have been offered a surprise of early mushrooms for supper, to have had all the glory of making two dollars and twenty-seven cents in a single day, and then to renounce it all and withdraw from these pleasant successes, needed much resolution. Literary employments are so vexed with uncertainties at best, and it was not until the voice of conscience sounded louder in my ears than the sea on the nearest pebble beach that I said unkind words of withdrawal to Mrs. Todd. She only became more wistfully affectionate than ever in her expressions, and looked as disappointed as I expected when I frankly told her that I could no longer enjoy the pleasure of what we called "seein' folks." I felt that I was cruel to a whole neighborhood in curtailing her liberty in this most important season for harvesting the different wild herbs that were so much counted upon to ease their winter ails.

"Well, dear," she said sorrowfully, "I've took great advantage o' your bein' here. I ain't had such a season for years, but I have never had nobody I could so trust. All you lack is a few qualities, but with time you'd gain judgment an' experience, an' be very able in the business. I'd stand right here an' say it to anybody."

Mrs. Todd and I were not separated or estranged by the change in our business relations; on the contrary, a deeper intimacy seemed to begin. I do not know what herb of the night it was that used sometimes to send out a penetrating odor late in the evening, after the dew had fallen, and the moon was high, and the cool air came up from the sea. Then Mrs. Todd would feel that she must talk to somebody, and I was only too glad to listen. We both fell under the spell, and she either stood outside the window, or made an errand to my sitting-room, and told, it might be very commonplace news of the day, or, as happened one misty summer night, all that lay deepest in her heart. It was in this way that I came to know that she had loved one who was far above her.

"No, dear, him I speak of could never think of me," she said. "When we was young together his mother didn't favor the match, an' done everything she could to part us; and folks thought we both married well, but't wa'n't what either one of us wanted most; an' now we're left alone again, an' might have had each other all the time. He was above bein' a seafarin' man, an' prospered more than most; he come of a high family, an' my lot was plain an' hard-workin'. I ain't seen him for some years; he's forgot our youthful feelin's, I expect, but a woman's heart is different; them feelin's comes back when you think you've done with 'em, as sure as spring comes with the year. An' I've always had ways of hearin' about him."

She stood in the centre of a braided rug, and its rings of black and gray seemed to circle about her feet in the dim light. Her height and massiveness in the low room gave her the look of a huge sibyl, while the strange fragrance of the mysterious herb blew in from the little garden.

III

The Schoolhouse

FOR SOME DAYS after this, Mrs. Todd's customers came and went past my windows, and, haying-time being nearly over, strangers began to arrive from the inland country, such was her widespread reputation. Sometimes I saw a pale young creature like a white windflower left over into midsummer, upon whose face consumption had set its bright and wistful mark; but oftener two stout, hard-worked women from the farms came together, and detailed their symptoms to Mrs. Todd in loud and cheerful voices, combining the satisfactions of a friendly gossip with the medical opportunity. They seemed to give much from their own store of therapeutic learning. I became aware of the school in which my landlady had strengthened her natural gift; but hers was always the governing mind, and the final command, "Take of hy'sop one handful" (or whatever herb it was), was received in respectful silence. One afternoon, when I had listened, — it was impossible not to listen, with cottonless ears, — and then laughed and listened again, with an idle pen in my hand, during a particularly spirited and personal conversation, I reached for my hat, and, taking blotting-book and all under my arm, I resolutely fled further temptation, and walked out past the fragrant green garden and up the dusty road. The way went straight uphill, and presently I stopped and turned to look back.

The tide was in, the wide harbor was surrounded by its dark woods, and the small wooden houses stood as near as they could get to the landing. Mrs. Todd's was the last house on the way inland. The gray ledges of the rocky shore were well covered with sod in most places, and the pasture bayberry and wild roses grew thick among them. I could see the higher inland country and the scattered farms. On the brink of the hill stood a little white schoolhouse, much wind-blown and weather-beaten, which was a landmark to seagoing folk; from its door there was a most beautiful view of sea and shore. The summer vacation now prevailed, and after finding the door unfastened, and taking a long look through one of the seaward windows, and reflecting afterward for some time in a shady place near by among the bayberry bushes, I returned to the chief place of business in the village, and, to the amusement of two of the selectmen, brothers and autocrats of Dunnet Landing, I hired the schoolhouse for the rest of the vacation for fifty cents a week.

Selfish as it may appear, the retired situation seemed to possess great advantages, and I spent many days there quite undisturbed, with the sea-breeze blowing through the small, high windows and swaying the heavy outside shutters to and fro. I hung my hat and luncheon-basket on an entry nail as if I were a small scholar, but I sat at the teacher's desk as if I were that great authority, with all the timid empty benches in rows before me. Now and then an idle sheep came and stood for a long time looking in at the door. At sundown I went back, feeling most busi-nesslike, down toward the village again, and usually met the flavor, not of the herb garden, but of Mrs. Todd's hot supper, halfway up the hill. On the nights when there were evening meetings or other public exercises that demanded her presence we had tea very early, and I was welcomed back as if from a long absence.

Once or twice I feigned excuses for staying at home, while Mrs. Todd made distant excursions, and came home late, with both hands full and a heavily laden apron. This was in pennyroyal time, and when the rare lobelia was in its prime and the elecampane was coming on. One day she appeared at the schoolhouse itself, partly out of amused curiosity about my industries; but she explained that there was no tansy in the neighborhood with such snap to it as some that grew about the school-house lot. Being scuffed down all the spring made it grow so much the better, like some folks that had it hard in their youth, and were bound to make the most of themselves before they died.

IV

At the Schoolhouse Window

ONE DAY I reached the schoolhouse very late, owing to attendance upon the funeral of an acquaintance and neighbor, with whose sad decline in health I had been familiar, and whose last days both the doctor and Mrs. Todd had tried in vain to ease. The services had taken place at one o'clock, and now, at quarter past two, I stood at the schoolhouse window, looking down at the procession as it went along the lower road close to the shore. It was a walking funeral, and even at that distance I could recognize most of the mourners as they went their solemn way. Mrs. Begg had been very much respected, and there was a large company of friends following to her grave. She had been brought up on one of the neighboring farms, and each of the few times that I had seen her she professed great dissatisfaction with town life. The people lived too close together for her liking, at the Landing, and she could not get used to the constant sound of the sea. She had lived to lament three seafaring husbands, and her house was decorated with West Indian curiosities, specimens of conch shells and fine coral which they had brought home from their voyages in lumber-laden ships. Mrs. Todd had told me all our neighbor's history. They had been girls together, and, to use her own phrase, had "both seen trouble till they knew the best and worst on 't." I could see the sorrowful, large figure of Mrs. Todd as I stood at the window. She made a break in the procession by walking slowly and keeping the after-part of it back. She held a handkerchief to her eyes, and I knew, with a pang of sympathy, that hers was not affected grief.

Beside her, after much difficulty, I recognized the one strange and unrelated person in all the company, an old man who had always been mysterious to me. I could see his thin, bending figure. He wore a narrow, long-tailed coat and walked with a stick, and had the same "cant to leeward" as the wind-bent trees on the height above.

This was Captain Littlepage, whom I had seen only once or twice before, sitting pale and old behind a closed window; never out of doors until now. Mrs. Todd always shook her head gravely when I asked a question, and said that he wasn't what he had been once, and seemed to class him with her other secrets. He might have belonged with a simple which grew in a certain slug-haunted corner of the garden, whose use she could never be betrayed into telling me, though I saw her cutting the tops by moonlight once, as if it were a charm, and not a medicine, like the great fading bloodroot leaves.

I could see that she was trying to keep pace with the old captain's lighter steps. He looked like an aged grasshopper of some strange human variety. Behind this pair was a short, impatient, little person, who kept the captain's house, and gave it what Mrs. Todd and others believed to be no proper sort of care. She was usually called "that Mari' Harris" in subdued conversation between intimates, but they treated her with anxious civility when they met her face to face.

The bay-sheltered islands and the great sea beyond stretched away to the far horizon southward and eastward; the little procession in the foreground looked futile and helpless on the edge of the rocky shore. It was a glorious day early in July, with a clear, high sky; there were no clouds, there was no noise of the sea. The song sparrows sang and sang, as if with joyous knowledge of immortality, and contempt for those who could so pettily concern themselves with death. I stood watching until the funeral procession had crept round a shoulder of the slope below and disappeared from the great landscape as if it had gone into a cave.

An hour later I was busy at my work. Now and then a bee blundered in and took me for an enemy; but there was a useful stick upon the teacher's desk, and I rapped to call the bees to order as if they were unruly scholars, or waved them away from their riots over the ink, which I had bought at the Landing store, and discovered too late to be scented with bergamot, as if to refresh the labors of anxious scribes. One anxious scribe felt very dull that day; a sheep-bell tinkled near by, and called her wandering wits after it. The sentences failed to catch these lovely summer cadences. For the first time I began to wish for a companion and for news from the outer world, which had been, half unconsciously, forgotten. Watching the funeral gave one a sort of pain. I began to wonder if I ought not to have walked with the rest, instead of hurrying away at the end of the services. Perhaps the Sunday gown I had put on for the occasion was making this disastrous change of feeling, but I had now made myself and my friends remember that I did not really belong to Dunnet Landing.

I sighed, and turned to the half-written page again.

V

Captain Littlepage

IT WAS A long time after this; an hour was very long in that coast town where nothing stole away the shortest minute. I had lost myself completely in work, when I heard footsteps outside. There was a steep footpath between the upper and the lower road, which I climbed to shorten the way, as the children had taught me, but I believed that Mrs. Todd would find it inaccessible, unless she had occasion to seek me in great haste. I wrote on, feeling like a besieged miser of time, while the footsteps came nearer, and the sheep-bell tinkled away in haste as if someone had shaken a stick in its wearer's face. Then I looked, and saw Captain Littlepage passing the nearest window; the next moment he tapped politely at the door.

"Come in, sir," I said, rising to meet him; and he entered, bowing with much courtesy. I stepped down from the desk and offered him a chair by the window, where he seated himself at once, being sadly spent by his climb. I returned to my fixed seat behind the teacher's desk, which gave him the lower place of a scholar.

"You ought to have the place of honor, Captain Littlepage," I said.

"A happy, rural seat of various views,"

he quoted, as he gazed out into the sunshine and up the long wooded shore. Then he glanced at me, and looked all about him as pleased as a child.

"My quotation was from Paradise Lost: the greatest of poems, I suppose you know?" and I nodded. "There 's nothing that ranks, to my mind, with Paradise Lost; it's all lofty, all lofty," he continued. "Shakespeare was a great poet; he copied life, but you have to put up with a great deal of low talk."

I now remembered that Mrs. Todd had told me one day that Captain Littlepage had overset his mind with too much reading; she had also made dark reference to his having "spells" of some unexplainable nature. I could not help wondering what errand had brought him out in search of me. There was something quite charming in his appearance: it was a face thin and delicate with refinement, but worn into appealing lines, as if he had suffered from loneliness and misapprehension. He

looked, with his careful precision of dress, as if he were the object of
cherishing care on the part of elderly unmarried sisters, but I knew Mari'
Harris to be a very common-place, inelegant person, who would have no
such standards; it was plain that the captain was his own attentive valet.
He sat looking at me expectantly. I could not help thinking that, with his
queer head and length of thinness, he was made to hop along the road of
life rather than to walk. The captain was very grave indeed, and I bade
my inward spirit keep close to discretion.

"Poor Mrs. Begg has gone," I ventured to say. I still wore my Sunday
gown by way of showing respect.

"She has gone," said the captain, — "very easy at the last, I was
informed; she slipped away as if she were glad of the opportunity."

I thought of the Countess of Carberry, and felt that history repeated
itself.

"She was one of the old stock," continued Captain Littlepage, with
touching sincerity. "She was very much looked up to in this town, and
will be missed."

I wondered, as I looked at him, if he had sprung from a line of
ministers; he had the refinement of look and air of command which are
the heritage of the old ecclesiastical families of New England. But as
Darwin says in his autobiography, "there is no such king as a sea-captain;
he is greater even than a king or a schoolmaster!"

Captain Littlepage moved his chair out of the wake of the sunshine,
and still sat looking at me. I began to be very eager to know upon what
errand he had come.

"It may be found out some o' these days," he said earnestly. "We may
know it all, the next step; where Mrs. Begg is now, for instance. Certainty, not conjecture, is what we all desire."

"I suppose we shall know it all some day," said I.

"We shall know it while yet below," insisted the captain, with a flush
of impatience on his thin cheeks. "We have not looked for truth in the
right direction. I know what I speak of; those who have laughed at me
little know how much reason my ideas are based upon." He waved his
hand toward the village below. "In that handful of houses they fancy that
they comprehend the universe."

I smiled, and waited for him to go on.

"I am an old man, as you can see," he continued, "and I have been a
shipmaster the greater part of my life, — forty-three years in all. You may
not think it, but I am above eighty years of age."

He did not look so old, and I hastened to say so.

"You must have left the sea a good many years ago, then, Captain
Littlepage?" I said.

"I should have been serviceable at least five or six years more," he answered. "My acquaintance with certain — my experience upon a certain occasion, I might say, gave rise to prejudice. I do not mind telling you that I chanced to learn of one of the greatest discoveries that man has ever made."

Now we were approaching dangerous ground, but a sudden sense of his sufferings at the hands of the ignorant came to my help, and I asked to hear more with all the deference I really felt. A swallow flew into the schoolhouse at this moment as if a kingbird were after it, and beat itself against the walls for a minute, and escaped again to the open air; but Captain Littlepage took no notice whatever of the flurry.

"I had a valuable cargo of general merchandise from the London docks to Fort Churchill, a station of the old company on Hudson's Bay," said the captain earnestly. "We were delayed in lading, and baffled by head winds and a heavy tumbling sea all the way north-about and across. Then the fog kept us off the coast; and when I made port at last, it was too late to delay in those northern waters with such a vessel and such a crew as I had. They cared for nothing, and idled me into a fit of sickness; but my first mate was a good, excellent man, with no more idea of being frozen in there until spring than I had, so we made what speed we could to get clear of Hudson's Bay and off the coast. I owned an eighth of the vessel, and he owned a sixteenth of her. She was a full-rigged ship, called the Minerva, but she was getting old and leaky. I meant it should be my last v'y'ge in her, and so it proved. She had been an excellent vessel in her day. Of the cowards aboard her I can't say so much."

"Then you were wrecked?" I asked, as he made a long pause.

"I wa'n't caught astern o' the lighter by any fault of mine," said the captain gloomily. "We left Fort Churchill and run out into the Bay with a light pair o' heels; but I had been vexed to death with their red-tape rigging at the company's office, and chilled with stayin' on deck an' tryin' to hurry up things, and when we were well out o' sight o' land, headin' for Hudson's Straits, I had a bad turn o' some sort o' fever, and had to stay below. The days were getting short, and we made good runs, all well on board but me, and the crew done their work by dint of hard driving."

I began to find this unexpected narrative a little dull. Captain Littlepage spoke with a kind of slow correctness that lacked the longshore high flavor to which I had grown used; but I listened respectfully while he explained the winds having become contrary, and talked on in a dreary sort of way about his voyage, the bad weather, and the disadvantages he was under in the lightness of his ship, which bounced about like a chip in a bucket, and would not answer the rudder or properly respond to the most careful setting of sails.

"So there we were blowin' along anyways," he complained; but looking at me at this moment, and seeing that my thoughts were unkindly wandering, he ceased to speak.

"It was a hard life at sea in those days, I am sure," said I, with redoubled interest.

"It was a dog's life," said the poor old gentleman, quite reassured, "but it made men of those who followed it. I see a change for the worse even in our own town here; full of loafers now, small and poor as 'tis, who once would have followed the sea, every lazy soul of 'em. There is no occupation so fit for just that class o' men who never get beyond the fo'cas'le. I view it, in addition, that a community narrows down and grows dreadful ignorant when it is shut up to its own affairs, and gets no knowledge of the outside world except from a cheap, unprincipled newspaper. In the old days, a good part o' the best men here knew a hundred ports and something of the way folks lived in them. They saw the world for themselves, and like's not their wives and children saw it with them. They may not have had the best of knowledge to carry with 'em sight-seein', but they were some acquainted with foreign lands an' their laws, an' could see outside the battle for town clerk here in Dunnet; they got some sense o' proportion. Yes, they lived more digni-fied, and their houses were better within an' without. Shipping's a terrible loss to this part o' New England from a social point o' view, ma'am."

"I have thought of that myself," I returned, with my interest quite awakened. "It accounts for the change in a great many things, — the sad disappearance of sea-captains, — doesn't it?"

"A shipmaster was apt to get the habit of reading," said my compan-ion, brightening still more, and taking on a most touching air of unre-serve. "A captain is not expected to be familiar with his crew, and for company's sake in dull days and nights he turns to his book. Most of us old shipmasters came to know 'most everything about something; one would take to readin' on farming topics, and some were great on medicine, — but Lord help their poor crews! — or some were all for history, and now and then there'd be one like me that gave his time to the poets. I was well acquainted with a shipmaster that was all for bees an' beekeepin'; and if you met him in port and went aboard, he'd sit and talk a terrible while about their havin' so much information, and the money that could be made out of keepin' 'em. He was one of the smartest captains that ever sailed the seas, but they used to call the

Newcastle, a great bark he commanded for many years, Tuttle's beehive.
There was old Cap'n Jameson: he had notions of Solomon's Temple,
and made a very handsome little model of the same, right from the
Scripture measurements, same's other sailors make little ships and
design new tricks of rigging and all that. No, there's nothing to take the
place of shipping in a place like ours. These bicycles offend me dread-
fully; they don't afford no real opportunities of experience such as a man
gained on a voyage. No: when folks left home in the old days they left it
to some purpose, and when they got home they stayed there and had
some pride in it. There's no large-minded way of thinking now: the worst
have got to be best and rule everything; we're all turned upside down
and going back year by year."

"Oh no, Captain Littlepage, I hope not," said I, trying to soothe his
feelings.

There was a silence in the schoolhouse, but we could hear the noise
of the water on a beach below. It sounded like the strange warning wave
that gives notice of the turn of the tide. A late golden robin, with the
most joyful and eager of voices, was singing close by in a thicket of wild
roses.

VI

The Waiting Place

"HOW DID YOU manage with the rest of that rough voyage on the
Minerva?" I asked.

"I shall be glad to explain to you," said Captain Littlepage, forgetting
his grievances for the moment. "If I had a map at hand I could explain
better. We were driven to and fro 'way up toward what we used to call
Parry's Discoveries, and lost our bearings. It was thick and foggy, and at
last I lost my ship; she drove on a rock, and we managed to get ashore on
what I took to be a barren island, the few of us that were left alive. When
she first struck, the sea was somewhat calmer than it had been, and most
of the crew, against orders, manned the long-boat and put off in a hurry,
and were never heard of more. Our own boat upset, but the carpenter
kept himself and me above water, and we drifted in. I had no strength to
call upon after my recent fever, and laid down to die; but he found the

tracks of a man and dog the second day, and got along the shore to one of those far missionary stations that the Moravians support. They were very poor themselves, and in distress; 'twas a useless place. There were but few Esquimaux left in that region. There we remained for some time, and I became acquainted with strange events."

The captain lifted his head and gave me a questioning glance. I could not help noticing that the dulled look in his eyes had gone, and there was instead a clear intentness that made them seem dark and piercing.

"There was a supply ship expected, and the pastor, an excellent Christian man, made no doubt that we should get passage in her. He was hoping that orders would come to break up the station; but every-thing was uncertain, and we got on the best we could for a while. We fished, and helped the people in other ways; there was no other way of paying our debts. I was taken to the pastor's house until I got better; but they were crowded, and I felt myself in the way, and made excuse to join with an old seaman, a Scotchman, who had built him a warm cabin, and had room in it for another. He was looked upon with regard, and had stood by the pastor in some troubles with the people. He had been on one of those English exploring parties that found one end of the road to the north pole, but never could find the other. We lived like dogs in a kennel, or so you'd thought if you had seen the hut from the outside; but the main thing was to keep warm; there were piles of bird-skins to lie on, and he'd made him a good bunk, and there was another for me. 'Twas dreadful dreary waitin' there; we begun to think the supply steamer was lost, and my poor ship broke up and strewed herself all along the shore. We got to watching on the headlands; my men and me knew the people were short of supplies and had to pinch themselves. It ought to read in the Bible, 'Man cannot live by fish alone,' if they'd told the truth of things; 'taint bread that wears the worst on you! First part of the time, old Gaffett, that I lived with, seemed speechless, and I didn't know what to make of him, nor he of me, I dare say; but as we got acquainted, I found he'd been through more disasters than I had, and had troubles that wa'n't going to let him live a great while. It used to ease his mind to talk to an understanding person, so we used to sit and talk together all day, if it rained or blew so that we couldn't get out. I'd got a bad blow on the back of my head at the time we came ashore, and it pained me at times, and my strength was broken, anyway; I've never been so able since."

Captain Littlepage fell into a reverie.

"Then I had the good of my reading," he explained presently. "I had no books; the pastor spoke but little English, and all his books were foreign; but I used to say over all I could remember. The old poets little

knew what comfort they could be to a man. I was well acquainted with
the works of Milton, but up there it did seem to me as if Shakespeare was
the king; he has his sea terms very accurate, and some beautiful passages
were calming to the mind. I could say them over until I shed tears; there
was nothing beautiful to me in that place but the stars above and those
passages of verse.

"Gaffett was always brooding and brooding, and talking to himself; he
was afraid he should never get away, and it preyed upon his mind. He
thought when I got home I could interest the scientific men in his
discovery: but they're all taken up with their own notions; some didn't
even take pains to answer the letters I wrote. You observe that I said this
crippled man Gaffett had been shipped on a voyage of discovery. I now
tell you that the ship was lost on its return, and only Gaffett and two
officers were saved off the Greenland coast, and he had knowledge later
that those men never got back to England; the brig they shipped on was
run down in the night. So no other living soul had the facts, and he gave
them to me. There is a strange sort of a country 'way up north beyond
the ice, and strange folks living in it. Gaffett believed it was the next
world to this."

"What do you mean, Captain Littlepage?" I exclaimed. The old man
was bending forward and whispering; he looked over his shoulder before
he spoke the last sentence.

"To hear old Gaffett tell about it was something awful," he said, going
on with his story quite steadily after the moment of excitement had
passed. " 'Twas first a tale of dogs and sledges, and cold and wind and
snow. Then they begun to find the ice grow rotten; they had been frozen
in, and got into a current flowing north, far up beyond Fox Channel,
and they took to their boats when the ship got crushed, and this warm
current took them out of sight of the ice, and into a great open sea; and
they still followed it due north, just the very way they had planned to go.
Then they struck a coast that wasn't laid down or charted, but the cliffs
were such that no boat could land until they found a bay and struck
across under sail to the other side where the shore looked lower; they
were scant of provisions and out of water, but they got sight of something
that looked like a great town. 'For God's sake, Gaffett!' said I, the first
time he told me. 'You don't mean a town two degrees farther north than
ships had ever been?' for he'd got their course marked on an old chart
that he'd pieced out at the top; but he insisted upon it, and told it over
and over again, to be sure I had it straight to carry to those who would be
interested. There was no snow and ice, he said, after they had sailed
some days with that warm current, which seemed to come right from

under the ice that they'd been pinched up in and had been crossing on foot for weeks."

"But what about the town?" I asked. "Did they get to the town?"

"They did," said the captain, "and found inhabitants; 'twas an awful condition of things. It appeared, as near as Gaffett could express it, like a place where there was neither living nor dead. They could see the place when they were approaching it by sea pretty near like any town, and thick with habitations; but all at once they lost sight of it altogether, and when they got close inshore they could see the shapes of folks, but they never could get near them, — all blowing gray figures that would pass along alone, or sometimes gathered in companies as if they were watching. The men were frightened at first, but the shapes never came near them, — it was as if they blew back; and at last they all got bold and went ashore, and found birds' eggs and sea fowl, like any wild northern spot where creatures were tame and folks had never been, and there was good water. Gaffett said that he and another man came near one o' the fog-shaped men that was going along slow with the look of a pack on his back, among the rocks, an' they chased him; but, Lord! he flittered away out o' sight like a leaf the wind takes with it, or a piece of cobweb. They would make as if they talked together, but there was no sound of voices, and 'they acted as if they didn't see us, but only felt us coming towards them,' says Gaffett one day, trying to tell the particulars. They couldn't see the town when they were ashore. One day the captain and the doctor were gone till night up across the high land where the town had seemed to be, and they came back at night beat out and white as ashes, and wrote and wrote all next day in their notebooks, and whispered together full of excitement, and they were sharp-spoken with the men when they offered to ask any questions.

"Then there came a day," said Captain Littlepage, leaning toward me with a strange look in his eyes, and whispering quickly. "The men all swore they wouldn't stay any longer; the man on watch early in the morning gave the alarm, and they all put off in the boat and got a little way out to sea. Those folks, or whatever they were, come about 'em like bats; all at once they raised incessant armies, and come as if to drive 'em back to sea. They stood thick at the edge o' the water like the ridges o' grim war; no thought o' flight, none of retreat. Sometimes a standing fight, then soaring on main wing tormented all the air. And when they'd got the boat out o' reach o' danger, Gaffett said they looked back, and there was the town again, standing up just as they'd seen it first, comin' on the coast. Say what you might, they all believed 'twas a kind of waiting-place between this world an' the next."

The captain had sprung to his feet in his excitement, and made excited gestures, but he still whispered huskily.

"Sit down, sir," I said as quietly as I could, and he sank into his chair quite spent.

"Gaffett thought the officers were hurrying home to report and to fit out a new expedition when they were all lost. At the time, the men got orders not to talk over what they had seen," the old man explained presently in a more natural tone.

"Weren't they all starving, and wasn't it a mirage or something of that sort?" I ventured to ask. But he looked at me blankly.

"Gaffett had got so that his mind ran on nothing else," he went on. "The ship's surgeon let fall an opinion to the captain, one day, that 'twas some condition o' the light and the magnetic currents that let them see those folks. 'Twa'n't a right-feeling part of the world, anyway; they had to battle with the compass to make it serve, an' everything seemed to go wrong. Gaffett had worked it out in his own mind that they was all common ghosts, but the conditions were unusual favorable for seeing them. He was always talking about the Ge'graphical Society, but he never took proper steps, as I viewed it now, and stayed right there at the mission. He was a good deal crippled, and thought they'd confine him in some jail of a hospital. He said he was waiting to find the right men to tell, somebody bound north. Once in a while they stopped there to leave a mail or something. He was set in his notions, and let two or three proper explorin' expeditions go by him because he didn't like their looks; but when I was there he had got restless, fearin' he might be taken away or something. He had all his directions written out straight as a string to give the right ones. I wanted him to trust 'em to me, so I might have something to show, but he wouldn't. I suppose he's dead now. I wrote to him an' I done all I could. 'Twill be a great exploit some o' these days."

I assented absent-mindedly, thinking more just then of my companion's alert, determined look and the seafaring, ready aspect that had come to his face; but at this moment there fell a sudden change, and the old, pathetic, scholarly look returned. Behind me hung a map of North America, and I saw, as I turned a little, that his eyes were fixed upon the northernmost regions and their careful recent outlines with a look of bewilderment.

VII

The Outer Island

GAFFETT WITH HIS good bunk and the bird-skins, the story of the wreck of the Minerva, the human-shaped creatures of fog and cobweb, the great words of Milton with which he described their onslaught upon the crew, all this moving tale had such an air of truth that I could not argue with Captain Littlepage. The old man looked away from the map as if it had vaguely troubled him, and regarded me appealingly.

"We were just speaking of" — and he stopped. I saw that he had suddenly forgotten his subject.

"There were a great many persons at the funeral," I hastened to say.

"Oh yes," the captain answered, with satisfaction. "All showed respect who could. The sad circumstances had for a moment slipped my mind. Yes, Mrs. Begg will be very much missed. She was a capital manager for her husband when he was at sea. Oh yes, shipping is a very great loss." And he sighed heavily. "There was hardly a man of any standing who didn't interest himself in some way in navigation. It always gave credit to a town. I call it low-water mark now here in Dunnet."

He rose with dignity to take leave, and asked me to stop at his house some day, when he would show me some outlandish things that he had brought home from sea. I was familiar with the subject of the decadence of shipping interests in all its affecting branches, having been already some time in Dunnet, and I felt sure that Captain Littlepage's mind had now returned to a safe level.

As we came down the hill toward the village our ways divided, and when I had seen the old captain well started on a smooth piece of sidewalk which would lead him to his own door, we parted, the best of friends. "Step in some afternoon," he said, as affectionately as if I were a fellow-shipmaster wrecked on the lee shore of age like himself. I turned toward home, and presently met Mrs. Todd coming toward me with an anxious expression.

"I see you sleevin' the old gentleman down the hill," she suggested.

"Yes. I've had a very interesting afternoon with him," I answered; and her face brightened.

"Oh, then he's all right. I was afraid 'twas one o' his flighty spells, an' Mari' Harris wouldn't" —

"Yes," I returned, smiling, "he has been telling me some old stories, but we talked about Mrs. Begg and the funeral beside, and Paradise Lost."

"I expect he got tellin' of you some o' his great narratives," she answered, looking at me shrewdly. "Funerals always sets him goin'. Some o' them tales hangs together toler'ble well," she added, with a sharper look than before. "An' he's been a great reader all his seafarin' days. Some thinks he overdid, and affected his head, but for a man o' his years he's amazin' now when he's at his best. Oh, he used to be a beautiful man!"

We were standing where there was a fine view of the harbor and its long stretches of shore all covered by the great army of the pointed firs, darkly cloaked and standing as if they waited to embark. As we looked far seaward among the outer islands, the trees seemed to march seaward still, going steadily over the heights and down to the water's edge.

It had been growing gray and cloudy, like the first evening of autumn, and a shadow had fallen on the darkening shore. Suddenly, as we looked, a gleam of golden sunshine struck the outer islands, and one of them shone out clear in the light, and revealed itself in a compelling way to our eyes. Mrs. Todd was looking off across the bay with a face full of affection and interest. The sunburst upon that outermost island made it seem like a sudden revelation of the world beyond this which some believe to be so near.

"That's where mother lives," said Mrs. Todd. "Can't we see it plain? I was brought up out there on Green Island. I know every rock an' bush on it."

"Your mother!" I exclaimed, with great interest.

"Yes, dear, cert'in; I've got her yet, old's I be. She's one of them spry, light-footed little women; always was, an' light-hearted, too," answered Mrs. Todd, with satisfaction. "She's seen all the trouble folks can see, without it's her last sickness; an' she's got a word of courage for everybody. Life ain't spoilt her a mite. She's eighty-six an' I'm sixty-seven, and I've seen the time I've felt a good sight the oldest. 'Land sakes alive!' says she, last time I was out to see her. 'How you do lurch about steppin' into a bo't?' I laughed so I liked to have gone right over into the water; an' we pushed off, an' left her laughin' there on the shore."

The light had faded as we watched. Mrs. Todd had mounted a gray rock, and stood there grand and architectural, like a *caryatide*. Presently she stepped down, and we continued our way homeward.

"You an' me, we'll take a bo't an' go out some day and see mother," she promised me. " 'Twould please her very much, an' there's one or two sca'ce herbs grows better on the island than anywheres else. I ain't seen their like nowheres here on the main."

"Now I'm goin' right down to get us each a mug o' my beer," she announced as we entered the house, "an' I believe I'll sneak in a little mite o' camomile. Goin' to the funeral an' all, I feel to have had a very wearin' afternoon."

I heard her going down into the cool little cellar, and then there was considerable delay. When she returned, mug in hand, I noticed the taste of camomile, in spite of my protest; but its flavor was disguised by some other herb that I did not know, and she stood over me until I drank it all and said that I liked it.

"I don't give that to everybody," said Mrs. Todd kindly; and I felt for a moment as if it were part of a spell and incantation, and as if my enchantress would now begin to look like the cobweb shapes of the arctic town. Nothing happened but a quiet evening and some delightful plans that we made about going to Green Island, and on the morrow there was the clear sunshine and blue sky of another day.

VIII

Green Island

ONE MORNING, very early, I heard Mrs. Todd in the garden outside my window. By the unusual loudness of her remarks to a passer-by, and the notes of a familiar hymn which she sang as she worked among the herbs, and which came as if directed purposely to the sleepy ears of my consciousness, I knew that she wished I would wake up and come and speak to her.

In a few minutes she responded to a morning voice from behind the blinds. "I expect you're goin' up to your schoolhouse to pass all this pleasant day; yes, I expect you're goin' to be dreadful busy," she said despairingly.

"Perhaps not," said I. "Why, what's going to be the matter with you, Mrs. Todd?" For I supposed that she was tempted by the fine weather to take one of her favorite expeditions along the shore pastures to gather herbs and simples, and would like to have me keep the house.

"No, I don't want to go nowhere by land," she answered gayly, — "no, not by land; but I don't know's we shall have a better day all the rest of the summer to go out to Green Island an' see mother. I waked up early thinkin' of her. The wind's light northeast, — 'twill take us right straight out; an' this time o' year it's liable to change round southwest an' fetch us home pretty, 'long late in the afternoon. Yes, it's goin' to be a good day."

"Speak to the captain and the Bowden boy, if you see anybody going by toward the landing," said I. "We'll take the big boat."

"Oh, my sakes! now you let me do things my way," said Mrs. Todd scornfully. "No, dear, we won't take no big bo't. I'll just git a handy dory, an' Johnny Bowden an' me, we'll man her ourselves. I don't want no abler bo't than a good dory, an' a nice light breeze ain't goin' to make no sea; an' Johnny's my cousin's son, — mother'll like to have him come; an' he'll be down to the herrin' weirs all the time we're there, anyway; we don't want to carry no men folks havin' to be considered every minute an' takin' up all our time. No, you let me do; we'll just slip out an' see mother by ourselves. I guess what breakfast you'll want's about ready now."

I had become well acquainted with Mrs. Todd as landlady, herb-gatherer, and rustic philosopher; we had been discreet fellow-passengers once or twice when I had sailed up the coast to a larger town than Dunnet Landing to do some shopping; but I was yet to become acquainted with her as a mariner. An hour later we pushed off from the landing in the desired dory. The tide was just on the turn, beginning to fall, and several friends and acquaintances stood along the side of the dilapidated wharf and cheered us by their words and evident interest. Johnny Bowden and I were both rowing in haste to get out where we could catch the breeze and put up the small sail which lay clumsily furled along the gunwale. Mrs. Todd sat aft, a stern and unbending lawgiver.

"You better let her drift; we'll get there 'bout as quick; the tide'll take her right out from under these old buildin's; there's plenty wind outside."

"Your bo't ain't trimmed proper, Mis' Todd!" exclaimed a voice from shore. "You're lo'ded so the bo't'll drag; you can't git her before the wind, ma'am. You set 'midships, Mis' Todd, an' let the boy hold the sheet 'n' steer after he gits the sail up; you won't never git out to Green Island that way. She's lo'ded bad, your bo't is, — she's heavy behind's she is now!"

Mrs. Todd turned with some difficulty and regarded the anxious adviser, my right oar flew out of water, and we seemed about to capsize.

"That you, Asa? Good-mornin'," she said politely. "I al'ays liked the starn seat best. When'd you git back from up country?"

This allusion to Asa's origin was not lost upon the rest of the company. We were some little distance from shore, but we could hear a chuckle of laughter, and Asa, a person who was too ready with his criticism and advice on every possible subject, turned and walked indignantly away.

When we caught the wind we were soon on our seaward course, and only stopped to underrun a trawl, for the floats of which Mrs. Todd looked earnestly, explaining that her mother might not be prepared for three extra to dinner; it was her brother's trawl, and she meant to just run her eye along for the right sort of a little haddock. I leaned over the boat's side with great interest and excitement, while she skillfully handled the long line of hooks, and made scornful remarks upon worthless, bait-consuming creatures of the sea as she reviewed them and left them on the trawl or shook them off into the waves. At last we came to what she pronounced a proper haddock, and having taken him on board and ended his life resolutely, we went our way.

As we sailed along I listened to an increasingly delightful commentary upon the islands, some of them barren rocks, or at best giving sparse pasturage for sheep in the early summer. On one of these an eager little flock ran to the water's edge and bleated at us so affectingly that I would willingly have stopped; but Mrs. Todd steered away from the rocks, and scolded at the sheep's mean owner, an acquaintance of hers, who grudged the little salt and still less care which the patient creatures needed. The hot midsummer sun makes prisons of these small islands that are a paradise in early June, with their cool springs and short thick-growing grass. On a larger island, farther out to sea, my entertaining companion showed me with glee the small houses of two farmers who shared the island between them, and declared that for three generations the people had not spoken to each other even in times of sickness or death or birth. "When the news come that the war was over, one of 'em knew it a week, and never stepped across his wall to tell the other," she said. "There, they enjoy it: they've got to have somethin' to interest 'em in such a place; 'tis a good deal more tryin' to be tied to folks you don't like than 'tis to be alone. Each of 'em tell the neighbors their wrongs; plenty likes to hear and tell again; them as fetch a bone'll carry one, an' so they keep the fight a-goin'. I must say I like variety myself; some folks washes Monday an' irons Tuesday the whole year round, even if the circus is goin' by!"

A long time before we landed at Green Island we could see the small white house, standing high like a beacon, where Mrs. Todd was born and where her mother lived, on a green slope above the water, with dark spruce woods still higher. There were crops in the fields, which we presently distinguished from one another. Mrs. Todd examined them while we were still far at sea. "Mother's late potatoes looks backward; ain't had rain enough so far," she pronounced her opinion. "They look weedier than what they call Front Street down to Cowper Centre. I expect brother William is so occupied with his herrin' weirs an' servin' out bait to the schooners that he don't think once a day of the land."

"What's the flag for, up above the spruces there behind the house?" I inquired, with eagerness.

"Oh, that's the sign for herrin'," she explained kindly, while Johnny Bowden regarded me with contemptuous surprise. "When they get enough for schooners they raise that flag; an' when 'tis a poor catch in the weir pocket they just fly a little signal down by the shore, an' then the small bo'ts comes and get enough an' over for their trawls. There, look! there she is: mother sees us; she's wavin' somethin' out o' the fore door! She'll be to the landin'-place quick's we are."

I looked, and could see a tiny flutter in the doorway, but a quicker signal had made its way from the heart on shore to the heart on the sea.

"How do you suppose she knows it is me?" said Mrs. Todd, with a tender smile on her broad face. "There, you never get over bein' a child long's you have a mother to go to. Look at the chimney, now; she's gone right in an' brightened up the fire. Well, there, I'm glad mother's well; you'll enjoy seein' her very much."

Mrs. Todd leaned back into her proper position, and the boat trimmed again. She took a firmer grasp of the sheet, and gave an impatient look up at the gaff and the leech of the little sail, and twitched the sheet as if she urged the wind like a horse. There came at once a fresh gust, and we seemed to have doubled our speed. Soon we were near enough to see a tiny figure with handkerchiefed head come down across the field and stand waiting for us at the cove above a curve of pebble beach.

Presently the dory grated on the pebbles, and Johnny Bowden, who had been kept in abeyance during the voyage, sprang out and used manful exertions to haul us up with the next wave, so that Mrs. Todd could make a dry landing.

"You done that very well," she said, mounting to her feet, and coming ashore somewhat stiffly, but with great dignity, refusing our outstretched hands, and returning to possess herself of a bag which had lain at her feet.

"Well, mother, here I be!" she announced with indifference; but they stood and beamed in each other's faces.

"Lookin' pretty well for an old lady, ain't she?" said Mrs. Todd's mother, turning away from her daughter to speak to me. She was a delightful little person herself, with bright eyes and an affectionate air of expectation like a child on a holiday. You felt as if Mrs. Blackett were an old and dear friend before you let go her cordial hand. We all started together up the hill.

"Now don't you haste too fast, mother," said Mrs. Todd warningly; " 'tis a far reach o' risin' ground to the fore door, and you won't set an' get your breath when you're once there, but go trotting about. Now don't you go a mite faster than we proceed with this bag an' basket. Johnny, there, 'll fetch up the haddock. I just made one stop to underrun William's trawl till I come to jes' such a fish's I thought you'd want to make one o' your nice chowders of. I've brought an onion with me that was layin' about on the window-sill at home."

"That's just what I was wantin'," said the hostess. "I give a sigh when you spoke o' chowder, knowin' my onions was out. William forgot to replenish us last time he was to the Landin'. Don't you haste so yourself, Almiry, up this risin' ground. I hear you commencin' to wheeze a'ready."

This mild revenge seemed to afford great pleasure to both giver and receiver. They laughed a little, and looked at each other affectionately, and then at me. Mrs. Todd considerately paused, and faced about to regard the wide sea view. I was glad to stop, being more out of breath than either of my companions, and I prolonged the halt by asking the names of the neighboring islands. There was a fine breeze blowing, which we felt more there on the high land than when we were running before it in the dory.

"Why, this ain't that kitten I saw when I was out last, the one that I said didn't appear likely?" exclaimed Mrs. Todd as we went our way.

"That's the one, Almiry," said her mother. "She always had a likely look to me, an' she's right after business. I never see such a mouser for one of her age. If't wan't for William, I never should have housed that other dronin' old thing so long; but he sets by her on account of her havin' a bob tail. I don't deem it advisable to maintain cats just on account of their havin' bob tails; they're like all other curiosities, good for them that wants to see 'm twice. This kitten catches mice for both, an' keeps me respectable as I ain't been for a year. She's a real understandin' little help, this kitten is. I picked her from among five Miss Augusta Pennell had over to Burnt Island," said the old woman, trudging along with the kitten close at her skirts. "Augusta, she says to me, 'Why,

Mis' Blackett, you've took the homeliest;' and, says I, 'I've got the smartest; I'm satisfied.'"

"I'd trust nobody sooner'n you to pick out a kitten, mother," said the daughter handsomely, and we went on in peace and harmony.

The house was just before us now, on a green level that looked as if a huge hand had scooped it out of the long green field we had been ascending. A little way above, the dark, spruce woods began to climb the top of the hill and cover the seaward slopes of the island. There was just room for the small farm and the forest; we looked down at the fish-house and its rough sheds, and the weirs stretching far out into the water. As we looked upward, the tops of the firs came sharp against the blue sky. There was a great stretch of rough pasture-land round the shoulder of the island to the eastward, and here were all the thick-scattered gray rocks that kept their places, and the gray backs of many sheep that forever wandered and fed on the thin sweet pasturage that fringed the ledges and made soft hollows and strips of green turf like growing velvet. I could see the rich green of bayberry bushes here and there, where the rocks made room. The air was very sweet; one could not help wishing to be a citizen of such a complete and tiny continent and home of fisherfolk.

The house was broad and clean, with a roof that looked heavy on its low walls. It was one of the houses that seem firm-rooted in the ground, as if they were two-thirds below the surface, like icebergs. The front door stood hospitably open in expectation of company, and an orderly vine grew at each side; but our path led to the kitchen door at the house-end, and there grew a mass of gay flowers and greenery, as if they had been swept together by some diligent garden broom into a tangled heap: there were portulacas all along under the lower step and straggling off into the grass, and clustering mallows that crept as near as they dared, like poor relations. I saw the bright eyes and brainless little heads of two half-grown chickens who were snuggled down among the mallows as if they had been chased away from the door more than once, and expected to be again.

"It seems kind o' formal comin' in this way," said Mrs. Todd impulsively, as we passed the flowers and came to the front doorstep; but she was mindful of the proprieties, and walked before us into the best room on the left.

"Why, mother, if you haven't gone an' turned the carpet!" she exclaimed, with something in her voice that spoke of awe and admiration. "When'd you get to it? I s'pose Mis' Addicks come over an' helped you, from White Island Landing?"

"No, she didn't," answered the old woman, standing proudly erect, and making the most of a great moment. "I done it all myself with William's help. He had a spare day, an' took right holt with me; an' 'twas all well beat on the grass, an' turned, an' put down again afore we went to bed. I ripped an' sewed over two o' them long breadths. I ain't had such a good night's sleep for two years."

"There, what do you think o' havin' such a mother as that for eighty-six year old?" said Mrs. Todd, standing before us like a large figure of Victory.

As for the mother, she took on a sudden look of youth; you felt as if she promised a great future, and was beginning, not ending, her summers and their happy toils.

"My, my!" exclaimed Mrs. Todd. "I couldn't ha' done it myself, I've got to own it."

"I was much pleased to have it off my mind," said Mrs. Blackett, humbly; "the more so because along at the first of the next week I wasn't very well. I suppose it may have been the change of weather."

Mrs. Todd could not resist a significant glance at me, but, with charming sympathy, she forbore to point the lesson or to connect this illness with its apparent cause. She loomed larger than ever in the little old-fashioned best room, with its few pieces of good furniture and pictures of national interest. The green paper curtains were stamped with conventional landscapes of a foreign order, — castles on inaccessible crags, and lovely lakes with steep wooded shores; under-foot the treasured carpet was covered thick with home-made rugs. There were empty glass lamps and crystallized bouquets of grass and some fine shells on the narrow mantelpiece.

"I was married in this room," said Mrs. Todd unexpectedly; and I heard her give a sigh after she had spoken, as if she could not help the touch of regret that would forever come with all her thoughts of happiness.

"We stood right there between the windows," she added, "and the minister stood here. William wouldn't come in. He was always odd about seein' folks, just's he is now. I run to meet 'em from a child, an' William, he'd take an' run away."

"I've been the gainer," said the old mother cheerfully. "William has been son an' daughter both since you was married off the island. He's been 'most too satisfied to stop at home 'long o' his old mother, but I always tell 'em I'm the gainer."

We were all moving toward the kitchen as if by common instinct. The best room was too suggestive of serious occasions, and the shades were all pulled down to shut out the summer light and air. It was indeed a tribute to Society to find a room set apart for her behests out there on so apparently neighborless and remote an island. Afternoon visits and evening festivals must be few in such a bleak situation at certain seasons of the year, but Mrs. Blackett was of those who do not live to themselves, and who have long since passed the line that divides mere self-concern from a valued share in whatever Society can give and take. There were those of her neighbors who never had taken the trouble to furnish a best room, but Mrs. Blackett was one who knew the uses of a parlor.

"Yes, do come right out into the old kitchen; I shan't make any stranger of you," she invited us pleasantly, after we had been properly received in the room appointed to formality. "I expect Almiry, here, 'll be driftin' out 'mongst the pasture-weeds quick's she can find a good excuse. 'Tis hot now. You'd better content yourselves till you get nice an' rested, an' 'long after dinner the sea-breeze 'll spring up, an' then you can take your walks, an' go up an' see the prospect from the big ledge. Almiry'll want to show off everything there is. Then I'll get you a good cup o' tea before you start to go home. The days are plenty long now."

While we were talking in the best room the selected fish had been mysteriously brought up from the shore, and lay all cleaned and ready in an earthen crock on the table.

"I think William might have just stopped an' said a word," remarked Mrs. Todd, pouting with high affront as she caught sight of it. "He's friendly enough when he comes ashore, an' was remarkable social the last time, for him."

"He ain't disposed to be very social with the ladies," explained William's mother, with a delightful glance at me, as if she counted upon my friendship and tolerance. "He's very particular, and he's all in his old fishin'-clothes to-day. He'll want me to tell him everything you said and done, after you've gone. William has very deep affections. He'll want to see you, Almiry. Yes, I guess he'll be in by an' by."

"I'll search for him by 'n' by, if he don't," proclaimed Mrs. Todd, with an air of unalterable resolution. "I know all of his burrows down 'long the shore. I'll catch him by hand 'fore he knows it. I've got some business with William, anyway. I brought forty-two cents with me that was due him for them last lobsters he brought in."

"You can leave it with me," suggested the little old mother, who was already stepping about among her pots and pans in the pantry, and preparing to make the chowder.

I became possessed of a sudden unwonted curiosity in regard to William, and felt that half the pleasure of my visit would be lost if I could not make his interesting acquaintance.

IX

William

MRS. TODD HAD taken the onion out of her basket and laid it down upon the kitchen table. "There's Johnny Bowden come with us, you know," she reminded her mother. "He'll be hungry enough to eat his size."

"I've got new doughnuts, dear," said the little old lady. "You don't often catch William 'n' me out o' provisions. I expect you might have chose a somewhat larger fish, but I'll try an' make it do. I shall have to have a few extra potatoes, but there's a field full out there, an' the hoe's leanin' against the well-house, in 'mongst the climbin'-beans." She smiled, and gave her daughter a commanding nod.

"Land sakes alive! Le's blow the horn for William," insisted Mrs. Todd, with some excitement. "He needn't break his spirit so far's to come in. He'll know you need him for something particular, an' then we can call to him as he comes up the path. I won't put him to no pain."

Mrs. Blackett's old face, for the first time, wore a look of trouble, and I found it necessary to counteract the teasing spirit of Almira. It was too pleasant to stay indoors altogether, even in such rewarding companionship; besides, I might meet William; and, straying out presently, I found the hoe by the well-house and an old splint basket at the woodshed door, and also found my way down to the field where there was a great square patch of rough, weedy potato-tops and tall ragweed. One corner was already dug, and I chose a fat-looking hill where the tops were well withered. There is all the pleasure that one can have in gold-digging in finding one's hopes satisfied in the riches of a good hill of potatoes. I longed to go on; but it did not seem frugal to dig any longer after my basket was full, and at last I took my hoe by the middle and lifted the basket to go back up the hill. I was sure that Mrs. Blackett must be waiting impatiently to slice the potatoes into the chowder, layer after layer, with the fish.

"You let me take holt o' that basket, ma'am," said the pleasant, anxious voice behind me.

I turned, startled in the silence of the wide field, and saw an elderly man, bent in the shoulders as fishermen often are, gray-headed and clean-shaven, and with a timid air. It was William. He looked just like his mother, and I had been imagining that he was large and stout like his sister, Almira Todd; and, strange to say, my fancy had led me to picture him not far from thirty and a little loutish. It was necessary instead to pay William the respect due to age.

I accustomed myself to plain facts on the instant, and we said good-morning like old friends. The basket was really heavy, and I put the hoe through its handle and offered him one end; then we moved easily toward the house together, speaking of the fine weather and of mackerel which were reported to be striking in all about the bay. William had been out since three o'clock, and had taken an extra fare of fish. I could feel that Mrs. Todd's eyes were upon us as we approached the house, and although I fell behind in the narrow path, and let William take the basket alone and precede me at some little distance the rest of the way, I could plainly hear her greet him.

"Got round to comin' in, didn't you?" she inquired, with amusement. "Well, now, that's clever. Didn't know's I should see you to-day, William, an' I wanted to settle an account."

I felt somewhat disturbed and responsible, but when I joined them they were on most simple and friendly terms. It became evident that, with William, it was the first step that cost, and that, having once joined in social interests, he was able to pursue them with more or less pleasure. He was about sixty, and not young-looking for his years, yet so undying is the spirit of youth, and bashfulness has such a power of survival, that I felt all the time as if one must try to make the occasion easy for some one who was young and new to the affairs of social life. He asked politely if I would like to go up to the great ledge while dinner was getting ready; so, not without a deep sense of pleasure, and a delighted look of surprise from the two hostesses, we started, William and I, as if both of us felt much younger than we looked. Such was the innocence and simplicity of the moment that when I heard Mrs. Todd laughing behind us in the kitchen I laughed too, but William did not even blush. I think he was a little deaf, and he stepped along before me most businesslike and intent upon his errand.

We went from the upper edge of the field above the house into a smooth, brown path among the dark spruces. The hot sun brought out the fragrance of the pitchy bark, and the shade was pleasant as we

climbed the hill. William stopped once or twice to show me a great
wasps'-nest close by, or some fishhawks'-nests below in a bit of swamp.
He picked a few sprigs of late-blooming linnaea as we came out upon an
open bit of pasture at the top of the island, and gave them to me without
speaking, but he knew as well as I that one could not say half he wished
about linnaea. Through this piece of rough pasture ran a huge shape of
stone like the great backbone of an enormous creature. At the end, near
the woods, we could climb up on it and walk along to the highest point;
there above the circle of pointed firs we could look down over all the
island, and could see the ocean that circled this and a hundred other bits
of island ground, the mainland shore and all the far horizons. It gave a
sudden sense of space, for nothing stopped the eye or hedged one in, —
that sense of liberty in space and time which great prospects always give.

"There ain't no such view in the world, I expect," said William
proudly, and I hastened to speak my heartfelt tribute of praise; it was
impossible not to feel as if an untraveled boy had spoken, and yet one
loved to have him value his native heath.

X

Where Pennyroyal Grew

WE WERE A little late to dinner, but Mrs. Blackett and Mrs. Todd were
lenient, and we all took our places after William had paused to wash his
hands, like a pious Brahmin, at the well, and put on a neat blue coat
which he took from a peg behind the kitchen door. Then he resolutely
asked a blessing in words that I could not hear, and we ate the chowder
and were thankful. The kitten went round and round the table, quite
erect, and, holding on by her fierce young claws, she stopped to mew
with pathos at each elbow, or darted off to the open door when a song
sparrow forgot himself and lit in the grass too near. William did not talk
much, but his sister Todd occupied the time and told all the news there
was to tell of Dunnet Landing and its coasts, while the old mother
listened with delight. Her hospitality was something exquisite; she had
the gift which so many women lack, of being able to make themselves
and their houses belong entirely to a guest's pleasure, — that charming
surrender for the moment of themselves and whatever belongs to them,

so that they make a part of one's own life that can never be forgotten. Tact is after all a kind of mindreading, and my hostess held the golden gift. Sympathy is of the mind as well as the heart, and Mrs. Blackett's world and mine were one from the moment we met. Besides, she had that final, that highest gift of heaven, a perfect self-forgetfulness. Sometimes, as I watched her eager, sweet old face, I wondered why she had been set to shine on this lonely island of the northern coast. It must have been to keep the balance true, and make up to all her scattered and depending neighbors for other things which they may have lacked.

When we had finished clearing away the old blue plates, and the kitten had taken care of her share of the fresh haddock, just as we were putting back the kitchen chairs in their places, Mrs. Todd said briskly that she must go up into the pasture now to gather the desired herbs.

"You can stop here an' rest, or you can accompany me," she announced. "Mother ought to have her nap, and when we come back she an' William'll sing for you. She admires music," said Mrs. Todd, turning to speak to her mother.

But Mrs. Blackett tried to say that she couldn't sing as she used, and perhaps William wouldn't feel like it. She looked tired, the good old soul, or I should have liked to sit in the peaceful little house while she slept; I had had much pleasant experience of pastures already in her daughter's company. But it seemed best to go with Mrs. Todd, and off we went.

Mrs. Todd carried the gingham bag which she had brought from home, and a small heavy burden in the bottom made it hang straight and slender from her hand. The way was steep, and she soon grew breathless, so that we sat down to rest awhile on a convenient large stone among the bayberry.

"There, I wanted you to see this, — 'tis mother's picture," said Mrs. Todd; "'twas taken once when she was up to Portland soon after she was married. That's me," she added, opening another worn case, and displaying the full face of the cheerful child she looked like still in spite of being past sixty. "And here's William an' father together. I take after father, large and heavy, an' William is like mother's folks, short an' thin. He ought to have made something o' himself, bein' a man an' so like mother; but though he's been very steady to work, an' kept up the farm, an' done his fishin' too right along, he never had mother's snap an' power o' seein' things just as they be. He's got excellent judgment, too," meditated William's sister, but she could not arrive at any satisfactory decision upon what she evidently thought his failure in life. "I think it is well to see any one so happy an' makin' the most of life just as it falls to hand," she said as she began to put the daguerreotypes away again; but I reached out my hand to see her mother's once more, a most flowerlike face of a lovely young woman in quaint dress. There was in the eyes a look of anticipation and joy, a far-off look that sought the horizon; one often sees it in seafaring families, inherited by girls and boys alike from men who spend their lives at sea, and are always watching for distant sails or the first loom of the land. At sea there is nothing to be seen close by, and this has its counterpart in a sailor's character, in the large and brave and patient traits that are developed, the hopeful pleasantness that one loves so in a seafarer.

When the family pictures were wrapped again in a big handkerchief, we set forward in a narrow footpath and made our way to a lonely place that faced northward, where there was more pasturage and fewer bushes, and we went down to the edge of short grass above some rocky cliffs where the deep sea broke with a great noise, though the wind was down and the water looked quiet a little way from shore. Among the grass grew such pennyroyal as the rest of the world could not provide. There was a fine fragrance in the air as we gathered it sprig by sprig and stepped along carefully, and Mrs. Todd pressed her aromatic nosegay between her hands and offered it to me again and again.

"There's nothin' like it," she said; "oh no, there's no such pennyr'yal as this in the state of Maine. It's the right pattern of the plant, and all the rest I ever see is but an imitation. Don't it do you good?" And I answered with enthusiasm.

"There, dear, I never showed nobody else but mother where to find this place; 'tis kind of sainted to me. Nathan, my husband, an' I used to love this place when we was courtin', and" — she hesitated, and then spoke softly — "when he was lost, 'twas just off shore tryin' to get in by the short channel out there between Squaw Islands, right in sight o' this headland where we'd set an' made our plans all summer long."

I had never heard her speak of her husband before, but I felt that we were friends now since she had brought me to this place.

" 'Twas but a dream with us," Mrs. Todd said. "I knew it when he was gone. I knew it" — and she whispered as if she were at confession — "I knew it afore he started to go to sea. My heart was gone out o' my keepin' before I ever saw Nathan; but he loved me well, and he made me real happy, and he died before he ever knew what he'd had to know if we'd lived long together. 'Tis very strange about love. No, Nathan never found out, but my heart was troubled when I knew him first. There's more women likes to be loved than there is of those that loves. I spent some happy hours right here. I always liked Nathan, and he never knew. But this pennyr'yal always reminded me, as I'd sit and gather it and hear him talkin' — it always would remind me of — the other one."

She looked away from me, and presently rose and went on by herself. There was something lonely and solitary about her great determined shape. She might have been Antigone alone on the Theban plain. It is not often given in a noisy world to come to the places of great grief and silence. An absolute, archaic grief possessed this countrywoman; she seemed like a renewal of some historic soul, with her sorrows and the remoteness of a daily life busied with rustic simplicities and the scents of primeval herbs.

I was not incompetent at herb-gathering, and after a while, when I had sat long enough waking myself to new thoughts, and reading a page of remembrance with new pleasure, I gathered some bunches, as I was bound to do, and at last we met again higher up the shore, in the plain every-day world we had left behind when we went down to the penny-royal plot. As we walked together along the high edge of the field we saw a hundred sails about the bay and farther seaward; it was mid-afternoon or after, and the day was coming to an end.

"Yes, they 're all makin' towards the shore, — the small craft an' the lobster smacks an' all," said my companion. "We must spend a little time with mother now, just to have our tea, an' then put for home."

"No matter if we lose the wind at sundown; I can row in with Johnny," said I; and Mrs. Todd nodded reassuringly and kept to her steady plod, not quickening her gait even when we saw William come round the corner of the house as if to look for us, and wave his hand and disappear.

"Why, William's right on deck; I didn't know's we should see any more of him!" exclaimed Mrs. Todd. "Now mother'll put the kettle right on; she's got a good fire goin'." I too could see the blue smoke thicken, and then we both walked a little faster, while Mrs. Todd groped in her full bag of herbs to find the daguerreotypes and be ready to put them in their places.

XI

The Old Singers

WILLIAM WAS sitting on the side door step, and the old mother was busy making her tea; she gave into my hand an old flowered-glass tea-caddy.

"William thought you'd like to see this, when he was settin' the table.

My father brought it to my mother from the island of Tobago; an' here's a pair of beautiful mugs that came with it." She opened the glass door of a little cupboard beside the chimney. "These I call my best things, dear," she said. "You'd laugh to see how we enjoy 'em Sunday nights in winter: we have a real company tea 'stead o' livin' right along just the same, an' I make somethin' good for a s'prise an' put on some o' my preserves, an' we get a-talkin' together an' have real pleasant times."

Mrs. Todd laughed indulgently, and looked to see what I thought of such childishness.

"I wish I could be here some Sunday evening," said I.

"William an' me'll be talkin' about you an' thinkin' o' this nice day," said Mrs. Blackett affectionately, and she glanced at William, and he looked up bravely and nodded. I began to discover that he and his sister could not speak their deeper feelings before each other.

"Now I want you an' mother to sing," said Mrs. Todd abruptly, with an air of command, and I gave William much sympathy in his evident distress.

"After I've had my cup o' tea, dear," answered the old hostess cheerfully; and so we sat down and took our cups and made merry while they lasted. It was impossible not to wish to stay on forever at Green Island, and I could not help saying so.

"I'm very happy here, both winter an' summer," said old Mrs. Blackett. "William an' I never wish for any other home, do we, William? I'm glad you find it pleasant; I wish you'd come an' stay, dear, whenever you feel inclined. But here's Almiry; I always think Providence was kind to plot an' have her husband leave her a good house where she really belonged. She'd been very restless if she'd had to continue here on Green Island. You wanted more scope, didn't you, Almiry, an' to live in a large place where more things grew? Sometimes folks wonders that we don't live together; perhaps we shall some time," and a shadow of sadness and apprehension flitted across her face. "The time o' sickness an' failin' has got to come to all. But Almiry's got an herb that's good for everything." She smiled as she spoke, and looked bright again.

"There's some herb that's good for everybody, except for them that thinks they're sick when they ain't," announced Mrs. Todd, with a truly professional air of finality. "Come, William, let's have Sweet Home, an' then mother'll sing Cupid an' the Bee for us."

Then followed a most charming surprise. William mastered his timidity and began to sing. His voice was a little faint and frail, like the family daguerreotypes, but it was a tenor voice, and perfectly true and sweet. I have never heard Home, Sweet Home sung as touchingly and seriously as he sang it; he seemed to make it quite new; and when he paused for a moment at the end of the first line and began the next, the old mother joined him and they sang together, she missing only the higher notes, where he seemed to lend his voice to hers for the moment and carry on her very note and air. It was the silent man's real and only means of expression, and one could have listened forever, and have asked for more and more songs of old Scotch and English inheritance and the best that have lived from the ballad music of the war. Mrs. Todd kept time visibly, and sometimes audibly, with her ample foot. I saw the tears in her eyes sometimes, when I could see beyond the tears in mine. But at last the songs ended and the time came to say good-by; it was the end of a great pleasure.

Mrs. Blackett, the dear old lady, opened the door of her bedroom while Mrs. Todd was tying up the herb bag, and William had gone down to get the boat ready and to blow the horn for Johnny Bowden, who had joined a roving boat party who were off the shore lobstering.

I went to the door of the bedroom, and thought how pleasant it looked, with its pink-and-white patchwork quilt and the brown unpainted paneling of its woodwork.

"Come right in, dear," she said. "I want you to set down in my old quilted rockin'-chair there by the window; you'll say it's the prettiest view in the house. I set there a good deal to rest me and when I want to read."

There was a worn red Bible on the lightstand, and Mrs. Blackett's heavy silver-bowed glasses; her thimble was on the narrow windowledge, and folded carefully on the table was a thick striped-cotton shirt that she was making for her son. Those dear old fingers and their loving stitches, that heart which had made the most of everything that needed love! Here was the real home, the heart of the old house on Green Island! I sat in the rocking-chair, and felt that it was a place of peace, the little brown bedroom, and the quiet outlook upon field and sea and sky.

I looked up, and we understood each other without speaking. "I shall like to think o' your settin' here to-day," said Mrs. Blackett. "I want you to come again. It has been so pleasant for William."

The wind served us all the way home, and did not fall or let the sail slacken until we were close to the shore. We had a generous freight of lobsters in the boat, and new potatoes which William had put aboard, and what Mrs. Todd proudly called a full "kag" of prime number one salted mackerel; and when we landed we had to make business arrangements to have these conveyed to her house in a wheelbarrow.

I never shall forget the day at Green Island. The town of Dunnet Landing seemed large and noisy and oppressive as we came ashore.

Such is the power of contrast; for the village was so still that I could hear
the shy whippoorwills singing that night as I lay awake in my downstairs
bedroom, and the scent of Mrs. Todd's herb garden under the window
blew in again and again with every gentle rising of the seabreeze.

XII

A Strange Sail

EXCEPT FOR a few stray guests, islanders or from the inland country, to
whom Mrs. Todd offered the hospitalities of a single meal, we were quite
by ourselves all summer; and when there were signs of invasion, late in
July, and a certain Mrs. Fosdick appeared like a strange sail on the far
horizon, I suffered much from apprehension. I had been living in the
quaint little house with as much comfort and unconsciousness as if it
were a larger body, or a double shell, in whose simple convolutions Mrs.
Todd and I had secreted ourselves, until some wandering hermit crab of
a visitor marked the little spare room for her own. Perhaps now and then
a castaway on a lonely desert island dreads the thought of being rescued.
I heard of Mrs. Fosdick for the first time with a selfish sense of objection;
but after all, I was still vacation-tenant of the schoolhouse, where I could
always be alone, and it was impossible not to sympathize with Mrs.
Todd, who, in spite of some preliminary grumbling, was really delighted
with the prospect of entertaining an old friend.

For nearly a month we received occasional news of Mrs. Fosdick, who
seemed to be making a royal progress from house to house in the inland
neighborhood, after the fashion of Queen Elizabeth. One Sunday after
another came and went, disappointing Mrs. Todd in the hope of seeing
her guest at church and fixing the day for the great visit to begin; but
Mrs. Fosdick was not ready to commit herself to a date. An assurance of
"some time this week" was not sufficiently definite from a free-footed
housekeeper's point of view, and Mrs. Todd put aside all herb-gathering
plans, and went through the various stages of expectation, provocation,
and despair. At last she was ready to believe that Mrs. Fosdick must have
forgotten her promise and returned to her home, which was vaguely said
to be over Thomaston way. But one evening, just as the supper-table was
cleared and "readied up," and Mrs. Todd had put her large apron over

her head and stepped forth for an evening stroll in the garden, the unexpected happened. She heard the sound of wheels, and gave an excited cry to me, as I sat by the window, that Mrs. Fosdick was coming right up the street.

"She may not be considerate, but she's dreadful good company," said Mrs. Todd hastily, coming back a few steps from the neighborhood of the gate. "No, she ain't a mite considerate, but there's a small lobster left over from your tea; yes, it's a real mercy there's a lobster. Susan Fosdick might just as well have passed the compliment o' comin' an hour ago."

"Perhaps she has had her supper," I ventured to suggest, sharing the housekeeper's anxiety, and meekly conscious of an inconsiderate appetite for my own supper after a long expedition up the bay. There were so few emergencies of any sort at Dunnet Landing that this one appeared overwhelming.

"No, she's rode 'way over from Nahum Brayton's place. I expect they were busy on the farm, and couldn't spare the horse in proper season. You just sly out an' set the teakittle on again, dear, an' drop in a good han'ful o' chips; the fire's all alive. I'll take her right up to lay off her things, as she'll be occupied with explanations an' gettin' her bunnit off, so you'll have plenty o' time. She's one I shouldn't like to have find me unprepared."

Mrs. Fosdick was already at the gate, and Mrs. Todd now turned with an air of complete surprise and delight to welcome her.

"Why, Susan Fosdick," I heard her exclaim in a fine unhindered voice, as if she were calling across a field, "I come near giving of you up! I was afraid you'd gone an' 'portioned out my visit to somebody else. I s'pose you've been to supper?"

"Lor', no, I ain't, Almiry Todd," said Mrs. Fosdick cheerfully, as she turned, laden with bags and bundles, from making her adieux to the boy driver. "I ain't had a mite o' supper, dear. I've been lottin' all the way on a cup o' that best tea o' yourn, — some o' that Oolong you keep in the little chist. I don't want none o' your useful herbs."

"I keep that tea for ministers' folks," gayly responded Mrs. Todd. "Come right along in, Susan Fosdick. I declare if you ain't the same old sixpence!"

As they came up the walk together, laughing like girls, I fled, full of cares, to the kitchen, to brighten the fire and be sure that the lobster, sole dependence of a late supper, was well out of reach of the cat. There proved to be fine reserves of wild raspberries and bread and butter, so that I regained my composure, and waited impatiently for my own share of this illustrious visit to begin. There was an instant sense of high festivity in the evening air from the moment when our guest had so frankly demanded the Oolong tea.

The great moment arrived. I was formally presented at the stair-foot, and the two friends passed on to the kitchen, where I soon heard a hospitable clink of crockery and the brisk stirring of a tea-cup. I sat in my high-backed rocking-chair by the window in the front room with an unreasonable feeling of being left out, like the child who stood at the gate in Hans Andersen's story. Mrs. Fosdick did not look, at first sight, like a person of great social gifts. She was a serious-looking little bit of an old woman, with a birdlike nod of the head. I had often been told that she was the "best hand in the world to make a visit," — as if to visit were the highest of vocations; that everybody wished for her, while few could get her; and I saw that Mrs. Todd felt a comfortable sense of distinction in being favored with the company of this eminent person who "knew just how." It was certainly true that Mrs. Fosdick gave both her hostess and me a warm feeling of enjoyment and expectation, as if she had the power of social suggestion to all neighboring minds.

The two friends did not reappear for at least an hour. I could hear their busy voices, loud and low by turns, as they ranged from public to confidential topics. At last Mrs. Todd kindly remembered me and returned, giving my door a ceremonious knock before she stepped in, with the small visitor in her wake. She reached behind her and took Mrs. Fosdick's hand as if she were young and bashful, and gave her a gentle pull forward.

"There, I don't know whether you're goin' to take to each other or not; no, nobody can't tell whether you'll suit each other, but I expect you 'll get along some way, both having seen the world," said our affectionate hostess. "You can inform Mis' Fosdick how we found the folks out to Green Island the other day. She's always been well acquainted with mother. I'll slip out now an' put away the supper things an' set my bread to rise, if you 'll both excuse me. You can come out an' keep me company when you get ready, either or both." And Mrs. Todd, large and amiable, disappeared and left us.

Being furnished not only with a subject of conversation, but with a safe refuge in the kitchen in case of incompatibility, Mrs. Fosdick and I sat down, prepared to make the best of each other. I soon discovered that she, like many of the elder women of that coast, had spent a part of her life at sea, and was full of a good traveler's curiosity and enlightenment. By the time we thought it discreet to join our hostess we were already sincere friends.

You may speak of a visit's setting in as well as a tide's, and it was impossible, as Mrs. Todd whispered to me, not to be pleased at the way this visit was setting in; a new impulse and refreshing of the social currents and seldom visited bays of memory appeared to have begun. Mrs. Fosdick had been the mother of a large family of sons and daughters, — sailors and sailors' wives, — and most of them had died before her. I soon grew more or less acquainted with the histories of all their fortunes and misfortunes, and subjects of an intimate nature were no more withheld from my ears than if I had been a shell on the mantelpiece. Mrs. Fosdick was not without a touch of dignity and elegance; she was fashionable in her dress, but it was a curiously well-preserved provincial fashion of some years back. In a wider sphere one might have called her a woman of the world, with her unexpected bits of modern knowledge, but Mrs. Todd's wisdom was an intimation of truth itself. She might belong to any age, like an idyl of Theocritus; but while she always understood Mrs. Fosdick, that entertaining pilgrim could not always understand Mrs. Todd.

That very first evening my friends plunged into a borderless sea of reminiscences and personal news. Mrs. Fosdick had been staying with a family who owned the farm where she was born, and she had visited every sunny knoll and shady field corner; but when she said that it might be for the last time, I detected in her tone something expectant of the contradiction which Mrs. Todd promptly offered.

"Almiry," said Mrs. Fosdick, with sadness, "you may say what you like, but I am one of nine brothers and sisters brought up on the old place, and we're all dead but me."

"Your sister Dailey ain't gone, is she? Why, no, Louisa ain't gone!" exclaimed Mrs. Todd, with surprise. "Why, I never heard of that occurrence!"

"Yes'm; she passed away last October, in Lynn. She had made her distant home in Vermont State, but she was making a visit to her youngest daughter. Louisa was the only one of my family whose funeral I wasn't able to attend, but 'twas a mere accident. All the rest of us were settled right about home. I thought it was very slack of 'em in Lynn not to fetch her to the old place; but when I came to hear about it, I learned that they'd recently put up a very elegant monument, and my sister Dailey was always great for show. She'd just been out to see the monument the week before she was taken down, and admired it so much that they felt sure of her wishes."

"So she's really gone, and the funeral was up to Lynn!" repeated Mrs. Todd, as if to impress the sad fact upon her mind. "She was some years younger than we be, too. I recollect the first day she ever came to school;

'twas that first year mother sent me inshore to stay with aunt Topham's folks and get my schooling. You fetched little Louisa to school one Monday mornin' in a pink dress an' her long curls, and she set between you an' me, and got cryin' after a while, so the teacher sent us home with her at recess."

"She was scared of seeing so many children about her; there was only her and me and brother John at home then; the older boys were to sea with father, an' the rest of us wa'n't born," explained Mrs. Fosdick. "That next fall we all went to sea together. Mother was uncertain till the last minute, as one may say. The ship was waiting orders, but the baby that then was, was born just in time, and there was a long spell of extra bad weather, so mother got about again before they had to sail, an' we all went. I remember my clothes were all left ashore in the east chamber in a basket where mother'd took them out o' my chist o' drawers an' left 'em ready to carry aboard. She didn't have nothing aboard, of her own, that she wanted to cut up for me, so when my dress wore out she just put me into a spare suit o' John's, jacket and trousers. I wasn't but eight years old an' he was most seven and large of his age. Quick as we made a port she went right ashore an' fitted me out pretty, but we was bound for the East Indies and didn't put in anywhere for a good while. So I had quite a spell o' freedom. Mother made my new skirt long because I was growing, and I poked about the deck after that, real discouraged, feeling the hem at my heels every minute, and as if youth was past and gone. I liked the trousers best; I used to climb the riggin' with 'em and frighten mother till she said an' vowed she'd never take me to sea again."

I thought by the polite absent-minded smile on Mrs. Todd's face this was no new story.

"Little Louisa was a beautiful child; yes, I always thought Louisa was very pretty," Mrs. Todd said. "She was a dear little girl in those days. She favored your mother; the rest of you took after your father's folks."

"We did certain," agreed Mrs. Fosdick, rocking steadily. "There, it does seem so pleasant to talk with an old acquaintance that knows what you know. I see so many of these new folks nowadays, that seem to have neither past nor future. Conversation's got to have some root in the past, or else you've got to explain every remark you make, an' it wears a person out."

Mrs. Todd gave a funny little laugh. "Yes'm, old friends is always best, 'less you can catch a new one that's fit to make an old one out of," she said, and we gave an affectionate glance at each other which Mrs. Fosdick could not have understood, being the latest comer to the house.

XIII

Poor Joanna

ONE EVENING my ears caught a mysterious allusion which Mrs. Todd made to Shell-heap Island. It was a chilly night of cold northeasterly rain, and I made a fire for the first time in the Franklin stove in my room, and begged my two housemates to come in and keep me company. The weather had convinced Mrs. Todd that it was time to make a supply of cough-drops, and she had been bringing forth herbs from dark and dry hiding-places, until now the pungent dust and odor of them had re-solved themselves into one mighty flavor of spearmint that came from a simmering caldron of syrup in the kitchen. She called it done, and well done, and had ostentatiously left it to cool, and taken her knitting-work because Mrs. Fosdick was busy with hers. They sat in the two rocking-chairs, the small woman and the large one, but now and then I could see that Mrs. Todd's thoughts remained with the cough-drops. The time of gathering herbs was nearly over, but the time of syrups and cordials had begun.

The heat of the open fire made us a little drowsy, but something in the way Mrs. Todd spoke of Shell-heap Island waked my interest. I waited to see if she would say any more, and then took a roundabout way back to the subject by saying what was first in my mind: that I wished the Green Island family were there to spend the evening with us, — Mrs. Todd's mother and her brother William.

Mrs. Todd smiled, and drummed on the arm of the rocking-chair. "Might scare William to death," she warned me; and Mrs. Fosdick mentioned her intention of going out to Green Island to stay two or three days, if the wind didn't make too much sea.

"Where is Shell-heap Island?" I ventured to ask, seizing the opportunity.

"Bears nor'east somewheres about three miles from Green Island; right off-shore, I should call it about eight miles out," said Mrs. Todd. "You never was there, dear; 'tis off the thoroughfares, and a very bad place to land at best."

"I should think 'twas," agreed Mrs. Fosdick, smoothing down her black silk apron. " 'Tis a place worth visitin' when you once get there. Some o' the old folks was kind o' fearful about it. 'Twas 'counted a great place in old Indian times; you can pick up their stone tools 'most any time if you hunt about. There's a beautiful spring o' water, too. Yes, I remember when they used to tell queer stories about Shell-heap Island. Some said 'twas a great bangeing-place for the Indians, and an old chief resided there once that ruled the winds; and others said they'd always heard that once the Indians come down from up country an' left a captive there without any bo't, an' 'twas too far to swim across to Black Island, so called, an' he lived there till he perished."

"I've heard say he walked the island after that, and sharp-sighted folks could see him an' lose him like one o' them citizens Cap'n Littlepage was acquainted with up to the north pole," announced Mrs. Todd grimly. "Anyway, there was Indians — you can see their shell-heap that named the island; and I've heard myself that 'twas one o' their cannibal places, but I never could believe it. There never was no cannibals on the coast o' Maine. All the Indians o' these regions are tame-looking folks."

"Sakes alive, yes!" exclaimed Mrs. Fosdick. "Ought to see them painted savages I've seen when I was young out in the South Sea Islands! That was the time for folks to travel, 'way back in the old whalin' days!"

"Whalin' must have been dull for a lady, hardly ever makin' a lively port, and not takin' in any mixed cargoes," said Mrs. Todd. "I never desired to go a whalin' v'y'ge myself."

"I used to return feelin' very slack an' behind the times, 'tis true," explained Mrs. Fosdick, "but 'twas excitin', an' we always done extra well, and felt rich when we did get ashore. I liked the variety. There, how times have changed; how few seafarin' families there are left! What a lot o' queer folks there used to be about here, anyway, when we was young, Almiry. Everybody's just like everybody else, now; nobody to laugh about, and nobody to cry about."

It seemed to me that there were peculiarities of character in the region of Dunnet Landing yet, but I did not like to interrupt.

"Yes," said Mrs. Todd after a moment of meditation, "there was certain a good many curiosities of human natur' in this neighborhood years ago. There was more energy then, and in some the energy took a singular turn. In these days the young folks is all copy-cats, 'fraid to death they won't be all just alike; as for the old folks, they pray for the advantage o' bein' a little different."

"I ain't heard of a copy-cat this great many years," said Mrs. Fosdick, laughing; " 'twas a favorite term o' my grandfather's. No, I wa'n't think-ing o' those things, but of them strange straying creatur's that used to rove the country. You don't see them now, or the ones that used to hive away in their own houses with some strange notion or other."

I thought again of Captain Littlepage, but my companions were not reminded of his name; and there was brother William at Green Island, whom we all three knew.

"I was talking o' poor Joanna the other day. I hadn't thought of her for a great while," said Mrs. Fosdick abruptly. "Mis' Brayton an' I recalled her as we sat together sewing. She was one o' your peculiar persons, wa'n't she? Speaking of such persons," she turned to explain to me, "there was a sort of a nun or hermit person lived out there for years all alone on Shell-heap Island. Miss Joanna Todd, her name was, — a cousin o' Almiry's late husband."

I expressed my interest, but as I glanced at Mrs. Todd I saw that she was confused by sudden affectionate feeling and unmistakable desire for reticence.

"I never want to hear Joanna laughed about," she said anxiously.

"Nor I," answered Mrs. Fosdick reassuringly. "She was crossed in love, — that was all the matter to begin with; but as I look back, I can see that Joanna was one doomed from the first to fall into a melancholy. She retired from the world for good an' all, though she was a well-off woman. All she wanted was to get away from folks; she thought she wasn't fit to live with anybody, and wanted to be free. Shell-heap Island come to her from her father, and first thing folks knew she'd gone off out there to live, and left word she didn't want no company. 'Twas a bad place to get to, unless the wind an' tide were just right; 'twas hard work to make a landing."

"What time of year was this?" I asked.

"Very late in the summer," said Mrs. Fosdick. "No, I never could laugh at Joanna, as some did. She set everything by the young man, an' they were going to marry in about a month, when he got bewitched with a girl 'way up the bay, and married her, and went off to Massachusetts. He wasn't well thought of, — there were those who thought Joanna's money was what had tempted him; but she'd given him her whole heart, an' she wa'n't so young as she had been. All her hopes were built on marryin', an' havin' a real home and somebody to look to; she acted just like a bird when its nest is spoilt. The day after she heard the news she was in dreadful woe, but the next she came to herself very quiet, and took the horse and wagon, and drove fourteen miles to the lawyer's, and signed a paper givin' her half of the farm to her brother. They never had got along very well together, but he didn't want to sign it, till she acted so distressed that he gave in. Edward Todd's wife was a good woman, who felt very bad indeed, and used every argument with Joanna; but Joanna took a poor old boat that had been her father's and lo'ded in a few things, and off she put all alone, with a good land breeze, right out to sea. Edward Todd ran down to the beach, an' stood there cryin' like a boy to see her go, but she was out o' hearin'. She never stepped foot on the mainland again long as she lived."

"How large an island is it? How did she manage in winter?" I asked.

"Perhaps thirty acres, rocks and all," answered Mrs. Todd, taking up the story gravely. "There can't be much of it that the salt spray don't fly over in storms. No, 'tis a dreadful small place to make a world of; it has a different look from any of the other islands, but there's a sheltered cove on the south side, with mud-flats across one end of it at low water where there's excellent clams, and the big shell-heap keeps some o' the wind off a little house her father took the trouble to build when he was a young man. They said there was an old house built o' logs there before that, with a kind of natural cellar in the rock under it. He used to stay out there days to a time, and anchor a little sloop he had, and dig clams to fill it, and sail up to Portland. They said the dealers always gave him an extra price, the clams were so noted..Joanna used to go out and stay with him. They were always great companions, so she knew just what 'twas out there. There was a few sheep that belonged to her brother an' her, but she bargained for him to come and get them on the edge o' cold weather. Yes, she desired him to come for the sheep; an' his wife thought perhaps Joanna'd return, but he said no, an' lo'ded the bo't with warm things an' what he thought she'd need through the winter. He come home with the sheep an' left the other things by the house, but she never so much as looked out o' the window. She done it for a penance. She must have wanted to see Edward by that time."

Mrs. Fosdick was fidgeting with eagerness to speak.

"Some thought the first cold snap would set her ashore, but she always remained," concluded Mrs. Todd soberly.

"Talk about the men not having any curiosity!" exclaimed Mrs. Fosdick scornfully. "Why, the waters round Shell-heap Island were white with sails all that fall. 'Twas never called no great of a fishin'-ground before. Many of 'em made excuse to go ashore to get water at the spring; but at last she spoke to a bo't-load, very dignified and calm, and said that she'd like it better if they'd make a practice of getting water to Black Island or somewheres else and leave her alone, except in case of accident or trouble. But there was one man who had always set everything by her from a boy. He'd have married her if the other hadn't come about an' spoilt his chance, and he used to get close to the island, before light, on his way out fishin', and throw a little bundle way up the green slope front o' the house. His sister told me she happened to see, the first time, what a pretty choice he made o' useful things that a woman would feel lost without. He stood off fishin', and could see them in the grass all day, though sometimes she'd come out and walk right by them. There was other bo'ts near, out after mackerel. But early next morning his present was gone. He didn't presume too much, but once he took her a nice firkin o' things he got up to Portland, and when spring come he landed her a hen and chickens in a nice little coop. There was a good many old friends had Joanna on their minds."

"Yes," said Mrs. Todd, losing her sad reserve in the growing sympathy of these reminiscences. "How everybody used to notice whether there was smoke out of the chimney! The Black Island folks could see her with their spy-glass, and if they'd ever missed getting some sign o' life they'd have sent notice to her folks. But after the first year or two Joanna was more and more forgotten as an every-day charge. Folks lived very simple in those days, you know," she continued, as Mrs. Fosdick's knitting was taking much thought at the moment. "I expect there was always plenty of driftwood thrown up, and a poor failin' patch of spruces covered all the north side of the island, so she always had something to burn. She was very fond of workin' in the garden ashore, and that first summer she began to till the little field out there, and raised a nice parcel o' potatoes. She could fish, o' course, and there was all her clams an' lobsters. You can always live well in any wild place by the sea when you'd starve to death up country, except 'twas berry time. Joanna had berries out there, blackberries at least, and there was a few herbs in case she needed them. Mullein in great quantities and a plant o' wormwood I remember seeing once when I stayed there, long before she fled out to Shell-heap. Yes, I recall the wormwood, which is always a planted herb, so there must have been folks there before the Todds' day. A growin' bush makes the best gravestone; I expect that wormwood always stood for somebody's solemn monument. Catnip, too, is a very endurin' herb about an old place."

"But what I want to know is what she did for other things," interrupted Mrs. Fosdick. "Almiry, what did she do for clothin' when she needed to replenish, or risin' for her bread, or the piece-bag that no woman can live long without?"

"Or company," suggested Mrs. Todd. "Joanna was one that loved her friends. There must have been a terrible sight o' long winter evenin's that first year."

"There was her hens," suggested Mrs. Fosdick, after reviewing the melancholy situation. "She never wanted the sheep after that first season. There wa'n't no proper pasture for sheep after the June grass was past, and she ascertained the fact and couldn't bear to see them suffer;

but the chickens done well. I remember sailin' by one spring afternoon, an' seein' the coops out front o' the house in the sun. How long was it before you went out with the minister? You were the first ones that ever really got ashore to see Joanna."

I had been reflecting upon a state of society which admitted such personal freedom and a voluntary hermitage. There was something mediaeval in the behavior of poor Joanna Todd under a disappointment of the heart. The two women had drawn closer together, and were talking on, quite unconscious of a listener.

"Poor Joanna!" said Mrs. Todd again, and sadly shook her head as if there were things one could not speak about.

"I called her a great fool," declared Mrs. Fosdick, with spirit, "but I pitied her then, and I pity her far more now. Some other minister would have been a great help to her, — one that preached self-forgetfulness and doin' for others to cure our own ills; but Parson Dimmick was a vague person, well meanin', but very humb in his feelin's. I don't suppose at that troubled time Joanna could think of any way to mend her troubles except to run off and hide."

"Mother used to say she didn't see how Joanna lived without having nobody to do for, getting her own meals and tending her own poor self day in an' day out," said Mrs. Todd sorrowfully.

"There was the hens," repeated Mrs. Fosdick kindly. "I expect she soon came to makin' folks o' them. No, I never went to work to blame Joanna, as some did. She was full o' feeling, and her troubles hurt her more than she could bear. I see it all now as I couldn't when I was young."

"I suppose in old times they had their shut-up convents for just such folks," said Mrs. Todd, as if she and her friend had disagreed about Joanna once, and were now in happy harmony. She seemed to speak with new openness and freedom. "Oh yes, I was only too pleased when the Reverend Mr. Dimmick invited me to go out with him. He hadn't been very long in the place when Joanna left home and friends. 'Twas one day that next summer after she went, and I had been married early in the spring. He felt that he ought to go out and visit her. She was a member of the church, and might wish to have him consider her spiritual state. I wa'n't so sure o' that, but I always liked Joanna, and I'd come to be her cousin by marriage. Nathan an' I had conversed about goin' out to pay her a visit, but he got his chance to sail sooner'n he expected. He always thought everything of her, and last time he come home, knowing nothing of her change, he brought her a beautiful coral pin from a port he'd touched at somewheres up the Mediterranean. So I wrapped the little box in a nice piece of paper and put it in my pocket, and picked her a bunch of fresh lemon balm, and off we started."

Mrs. Fosdick laughed. "I remember hearin' about your trials on the v'y'ge," she said.

"Why, yes," continued Mrs. Todd in her company manner. "I picked her the balm, an' we started. Why, yes, Susan, the minister liked to have cost me my life that day. He would fasten the sheet, though I advised against it. He said the rope was rough an' cut his hand. There was a fresh breeze, an' he went on talking rather high flown, an' I felt some interested. All of a sudden there come up a gust, and he gave a screech and stood right up and called for help, 'way out there to sea. I knocked him right over into the bottom o' the bo't, getting by to catch hold of the sheet an' untie it. He wasn't but a little man; I helped him right up after the squall passed, and made a handsome apology to him, but he did act kind o' offended."

"I do think they ought not to settle them landlocked folks in parishes where they're liable to be on the water," insisted Mrs. Fosdick. "Think of the families in our parish that was scattered all about the bay, and what a sight o' sails you used to see, in Mr. Dimmick's day, standing across to the mainland on a pleasant Sunday morning, filled with church-going folks, all sure to want him some time or other! You couldn't find no doctor that would stand up in the boat and screech if a flaw struck her."

"Old Dr. Bennett had a beautiful sailboat, didn't he?" responded Mrs. Todd. "And how well he used to brave the weather! Mother always said that in time o' trouble that tall white sail used to look like an angel's wing comin' over the sea to them that was in pain. Well, there's a difference in gifts. Mr. Dimmick was not without light."

" 'Twas light o' the moon, then," snapped Mrs. Fosdick; "he was pompous enough, but I never could remember a single word he said. There, go on, Mis' Todd; I forget a great deal about that day you went to see poor Joanna."

"I felt she saw us coming, and knew us a great way off; yes, I seemed to feel it within me," said our friend, laying down her knitting. "I kept my seat, and took the bo't inshore without saying a word; there was a short channel that I was sure Mr. Dimmick wasn't acquainted with, and the tide was very low. She never came out to warn us off nor anything, and I thought, as I hauled the bo't up on a wave and let the Reverend Mr. Dimmick step out, that it was somethin' gained to be safe ashore. There was a little smoke out o' the chimney o' Joanna's house, and it did look sort of homelike and pleasant with wild mornin'-glory vines trained up; an' there was a plot o' flowers under the front window, portulacas and

things. I believe she'd made a garden once, when she was stopping there
with her father, and some things must have seeded in. It looked as if she
might have gone over to the other side of the island. 'Twas neat and
pretty all about the house, and a lovely day in July. We walked up from
the beach together very sedate, and I felt for poor Nathan's little pin to
see if 'twas safe in my dress pocket. All of a sudden Joanna come right to
the fore door and stood there, not sayin' a word."

XIV

The Hermitage

MY COMPANIONS and I had been so intent upon the subject of the
conversation that we had not heard any one open the gate, but at this
moment, above the noise of the rain, we heard a loud knocking. We
were all startled as we sat by the fire, and Mrs. Todd rose hastily and went
to answer the call, leaving her rocking-chair in violent motion. Mrs.
Fosdick and I heard an anxious voice at the door speaking of a sick child,
and Mrs. Todd's kind, motherly voice inviting the messenger in: then we
waited in silence. There was a sound of heavy dropping of rain from the
eaves, and the distant roar and undertone of the sea. My thoughts flew
back to the lonely woman on her outer island; what separation from
humankind she must have felt, what terror and sadness, even in a
summer storm like this!

"You send right after the doctor if she ain't better in half an hour," said
Mrs. Todd to her worried customer as they parted; and I felt a warm
sense of comfort in the evident resources of even so small a neighborhood, but for the poor hermit Joanna there was no neighbor on a winter
night.

"How did she look?" demanded Mrs. Fosdick, without preface, as
our large hostess returned to the little room with a mist about her from
standing long in the wet doorway, and the sudden draught of her
coming beat out the smoke and flame from the Franklin stove. "How did
poor Joanna look?"

"She was the same as ever, except I thought she looked smaller,"
answered Mrs. Todd after thinking a moment; perhaps it was only a last

considering thought about her patient. "Yes, she was just the same, and looked very nice, Joanna did. I had been married since she left home, an' she treated me like her own folks. I expected she'd look strange, with her hair turned gray in a night or somethin', but she wore a pretty gingham dress I'd often seen her wear before she went away; she must have kept it nice for best in the afternoons. She always had beautiful, quiet manners. I remember she waited till we were close to her, and then kissed me real affectionate, and inquired for Nathan before she shook hands with the minister, and then she invited us both in. 'Twas the same little house her father had built him when he was a bachelor, with one livin'-room, and a little mite of a bedroom out of it where she slept, but 'twas neat as a ship's cabin. There was some old chairs, an' a seat made of a long box that might have held boat tackle an' things to lock up in his fishin' days, and a good enough stove so anybody could cook and keep warm in cold weather. I went over once from home and stayed 'most a week with Joanna when we was girls, and those young happy days rose up before me. Her father was busy all day fishin' or clammin'; he was one o' the pleasantest men in the world, but Joanna's mother had the grim streak, and never knew what 'twas to be happy. The first minute my eyes fell upon Joanna's face that day I saw how she had grown to look like Mis' Todd. 'Twas the mother right over again."

"Oh dear me!" said Mrs. Fosdick.

"Joanna had done one thing very pretty. There was a little piece o' swamp on the island where good rushes grew plenty, and she'd gathered 'em, and braided some beautiful mats for the floor and a thick cushion for the long bunk. She'd showed a good deal of invention; you see there was a nice chance to pick up pieces o' wood and boards that drove ashore, and she'd made good use o' what she found. There wasn't no clock, but she had a few dishes on a shelf, and flowers set about in shells fixed to the walls, so it did look sort of homelike, though so lonely and poor. I couldn't keep the tears out o' my eyes, I felt so sad. I said to myself, I must get mother to come over an' see Joanna; the love in mother's heart would warm her, an' she might be able to advise."

"Oh no, Joanna was dreadful stern," said Mrs. Fosdick.

"We were all settin' down very proper, but Joanna would keep stealin' glances at me as if she was glad I come. She had but little to say; she was real polite an' gentle, and yet forbiddin'. The minister found it hard," confessed Mrs. Todd; "he got embarrassed, an' when he put on his authority and asked her if she felt to enjoy religion in her present situation, an' she replied that she must be excused from answerin', I thought I should fly. She might have made it easier for him; after all, he was the minister and had taken some trouble to come out, though 'twas kind of cold an' unfeelin' the way he inquired. I thought he might have seen the little old Bible a-layin' on the shelf close by him, an' I wished he knew enough to just lay his hand on it an' read somethin' kind an' fatherly 'stead of accusin' her, an' then given poor Joanna his blessin' with the hope she might be led to comfort. He did offer prayer, but 'twas all about hearin' the voice o' God out o' the whirlwind; and I thought while he was goin' on that anybody that had spent the long cold winter all alone out on Shell-heap Island knew a good deal more about those things than he did. I got so provoked I opened my eyes and stared right at him.

"She didn't take no notice, she kep' a nice respectful manner towards him, and when there come a pause she asked if he had any interest about the old Indian remains, and took down some queer stone gouges and hammers off of one of her shelves and showed them to him same's if he was a boy. He remarked that he'd like to walk over an' see the shell-heap; so she went right to the door and pointed him the way. I see then that she'd made her some kind o' sandal-shoes out o' the fine rushes to wear on her feet; she stepped light an' nice in 'em as shoes."

Mrs. Fosdick leaned back in her rocking-chair and gave a heavy sigh.

"I didn't move at first, but I'd held out just as long as I could," said Mrs. Todd, whose voice trembled a little. "When Joanna returned from the door, an' I could see that man's stupid back departin' among the wild rose bushes, I just ran to her an' caught her in my arms. I wasn't so big as I be now, and she was older than me, but I hugged her tight, just as if she was a child. 'Oh, Joanna dear,' I says, 'won't you come ashore an' live 'long o' me at the Landin', or go over to Green Island to mother's when winter comes? Nobody shall trouble you, an' mother finds it hard bein' alone. I can't bear to leave you here' — and I burst right out crying. I'd had my own trials, young as I was, an' she knew it. Oh, I did entreat her; yes, I entreated Joanna."

"What did she say then?" asked Mrs. Fosdick, much moved.

"She looked the same way, sad an' remote through it all," said Mrs. Todd mournfully. "She took hold of my hand, and we sat down close together; 'twas as if she turned round an' made a child of me. 'I haven't got no right to live with folks no more,' she said. 'You must never ask me again, Almiry: I've done the only thing I could do, and I've made my choice. I feel a great comfort in your kindness, but I don't deserve it. I have committed the unpardonable sin; you don't understand,' says she humbly. 'I was in great wrath and trouble, and my thoughts was so wicked towards God that I can't expect ever to be forgiven. I have come to know what it is to have patience, but I have lost my hope. You must tell those that ask how 'tis with me,' she said, 'an' tell them I want to be alone.' I couldn't speak; no, there wa'n't anything I could say, she seemed so above everything common. I was a good deal younger then than I be now, and I got Nathan's little coral pin out o' my pocket and put it into her hand; and when she saw it and I told her where it come from, her face did really light up for a minute, sort of bright an' pleasant. 'Nathan an' I was always good friends; I'm glad he don't think hard of me,' says she. 'I want you to have it, Almiry, an' wear it for love o' both o' us,' and she handed it back to me. 'You give my love to Nathan, — he's a dear good man,' she said; 'an' tell your mother, if I should be sick she mustn't wish I could get well, but I want her to be the one to come.' Then she seemed to have said all she wanted to, as if she was done with the world, and we sat there a few minutes longer together. It was real sweet and quiet except for a good many birds and the sea rollin' up on the beach; but at last she rose, an' I did too, and she kissed me and held my hand in hers a minute, as if to say good-by; then she turned and went right away out o' the door and disappeared.

"The minister come back pretty soon, and I told him I was all ready, and we started down to the bo't. He had picked up some round stones and things and was carrying them in his pocket-handkerchief; an' he sat down amidships without making any question, and let me take the rudder an' work the bo't, an' made no remarks for some time, until we sort of eased it off speaking of the weather, an' subjects that arose as we skirted Black Island, where two or three families lived belongin' to the parish. He preached next Sabbath as usual, somethin' high soundin' about the creation, and I couldn't help thinkin' he might never get no further; he seemed to know no remedies, but he had a great use of words."

Mrs. Fosdick sighed again. "Hearin' you tell about Joanna brings the time right back as if 'twas yesterday," she said. "Yes, she was one o' them poor things that talked about the great sin; we don't seem to hear nothing about the unpardonable sin now, but you may say 'twas not uncommon then."

"I expect that if it had been in these days, such a person would be plagued to death with idle folks," continued Mrs. Todd, after a long pause. "As it was, nobody trespassed on her; all the folks about the bay respected her an' her feelings; but as time wore on, after you left here, one after another ventured to make occasion to put somethin' ashore for her if they went that way. I know mother used to go to see her some-times, and send William over now and then with something fresh an' nice from the farm. There is a point on the sheltered side where you can lay a boat close to shore an' land anything safe on the turf out o' reach o' the water. There were one or two others, old folks, that she would see, and now an' then she'd hail a passin' boat an' ask for somethin'; and mother got her to promise that she would make some sign to the Black Island folks if she wanted help. I never saw her myself to speak to after that day."

"I expect nowadays, if such a thing happened, she'd have gone out West to her uncle's folks or up to Massachusetts and had a change, an' come home good as new. The world's bigger an' freer than it used to be," urged Mrs. Fosdick.

"No," said her friend. " 'Tis like bad eyesight, the mind of such a person: if your eyes don't see right there may be a remedy, but there's no kind of glasses to remedy the mind. No, Joanna was Joanna, and there she lays on her island where she lived and did her poor penance. She told mother the day she was dyin' that she always used to want to be fetched inshore when it come to the last; but she'd thought it over, and desired to be laid on the island, if 'twas thought right. So the funeral was out there, a Saturday afternoon in September. 'Twas a pretty day, and there wa'n't hardly a boat on the coast within twenty miles that didn't head for Shell-heap cram-full o' folks an' all real respectful, same's if she'd always stayed ashore and held her friends. Some went out o' mere curiosity, I don't doubt, — there's always such to every funeral; but most had real feelin', and went purpose to show it. She'd got most o' the wild sparrows as tame as could be, livin' out there so long among 'em, and one flew right in and lit on the coffin an' begun to sing while Mr. Dimmick was speakin'. He was put out by it, an' acted as if he didn't know whether to stop or go on. I may have been prejudiced, but I wa'n't the only one thought the poor little bird done the best of the two."

"What became o' the man that treated her so, did you ever hear?" asked Mrs. Fosdick. "I know he lived up to Massachusetts for a while. Somebody who came from the same place told me that he was in trade there an' doin' very well, but that was years ago."

"I never heard anything more than that; he went to the war in one o' the early regiments. No, I never heard any more of him," answered Mrs. Todd. "Joanna was another sort of person, and perhaps he showed good judgment in marryin' somebody else, if only he'd behaved straight-forward and manly. He was a shifty-eyed, coaxin' sort of man, that got what he wanted out o' folks, an' only gave when he wanted to buy, made friends easy and lost 'em without knowin' the difference. She'd had a piece o' work tryin' to make him walk accordin' to her

right ideas, but she'd have had too much variety ever to fall into a
melancholy. Some is meant to be the Joannas in this world, an' 'twas
her poor lot."

XV

On Shell-heap Island

SOME TIME AFTER Mrs. Fosdick's visit was over and we had returned to
our former quietness, I was out sailing alone with Captain Bowden in
his large boat. We were taking the crooked northeasterly channel seaward, and were well out from shore while it was still early in the
afternoon. I found myself presently among some unfamiliar islands, and
suddenly remembered the story of poor Joanna. There is something in
the fact of a hermitage that cannot fail to touch the imagination; the
recluses are a sad kindred, but they are never commonplace. Mrs. Todd
had truly said that Joanna was like one of the saints in the desert; the
loneliness of sorrow will forever keep alive their sad succession.

"Where is Shell-heap Island?" I asked eagerly.

"You see Shell-heap now, layin' 'way out beyond Black Island there,"
answered the captain, pointing with outstretched arm as he stood, and
holding the rudder with his knee.

"I should like very much to go there," said I, and the captain, without
comment, changed his course a little more to the eastward and let the
reef out of his mainsail.

"I don't know's we can make an easy landin' for ye," he remarked
doubtfully. "May get your feet wet; bad place to land. Trouble is I ought
to have brought a tag-boat; but they clutch on to the water so, an' I do
love to sail free. This gre't boat gets easy bothered with anything trailin'.
'Tain't breakin' much on the meetin'-house ledges; guess I can fetch in
to Shell-heap."

"How long is it since Miss Joanna Todd died?" I asked, partly by way of
explanation.

"Twenty-two years come September," answered the captain, after
reflection. "She died the same year as my oldest boy was born, an' the
town house was burnt over to the Port. I didn't know but you merely
wanted to hunt for some o' them Indian relics. Long's you want to see

where Joanna lived — No, 'tain't breakin' over the ledges; we'll manage to fetch across the shoals somehow, 'tis such a distance to go 'way round, and tide's a-risin'," he ended hopefully, and we sailed steadily on, the captain speechless with intent watching of a difficult course, until the small island with its low whitish promontory lay in full view before us under the bright afternoon sun.

The month was August, and I had seen the color of the islands change from the fresh green of June to a sunburnt brown that made them look like stone, except where the dark green of the spruces and fir balsam kept the tint that even winter storms might deepen, but not fade. The few wind-bent trees on Shell-heap Island were mostly dead and gray, but there were some low-growing bushes, and a stripe of light green ran along just above the shore, which I knew to be wild morning-glories. As we came close I could see the high stone walls of a small square field, though there were no sheep left to assail it; and below, there was a little harbor-like cove where Captain Bowden was boldly running the great boat in to seek a landing-place. There was a crooked channel of deep water which led close up against the shore.

"There, you hold fast for'ard there, an' wait for her to lift on the wave. You'll make a good landin' if you're smart; right on the port-hand side!" the captain called excitedly; and I, standing ready with high ambition, seized my chance and leaped over to the grassy bank.

"I'm beat if I ain't aground after all!" mourned the captain despondently.

But I could reach the bowsprit, and he pushed with the boat-hook, while the wind veered round a little as if on purpose and helped with the sail; so presently the boat was free and began to drift out from shore.

"Used to call this p'int Joanna's wharf privilege, but 't has worn away in the weather since her time. I thought one or two bumps wouldn't hurt us none, — paint's got to be renewed, anyway, — but I never thought she'd tetch. I figured on shyin' by," the captain apologized. "She's too gre't a boat to handle well in here; but I used to sort of shy by in Joanna's day, an' cast a little somethin' ashore — some apples or a couple o' pears if I had 'em — on the grass, where she'd be sure to see."

I stood watching while Captain Bowden cleverly found his way back to deeper water. "You needn't make no haste," he called to me; "I'll keep within call. Joanna lays right up there in the far corner o' the field. There used to be a path led to the place. I always knew her well. I was out here to the funeral."

I found the path; it was touching to discover that this lonely spot was not without its pilgrims. Later generations will know less and less of Joanna herself, but there are paths trodden to the shrines of solitude the world over, — the world cannot forget them, try as it may; the feet of the young find them out because of curiosity and dim foreboding; while the old bring hearts full of remembrance. This plain anchorite had been one of those whom sorrow made too lonely to brave the sight of men, too timid to front the simple world she knew, yet valiant enough to live alone with her poor insistent human nature and the calms and passions of the sea and sky.

The birds were flying all about the field; they fluttered up out of the grass at my feet as I walked along, so tame that I liked to think they kept some happy tradition from summer to summer of the safety of nests and good fellowship of mankind. Poor Joanna's house was gone except the stones of its foundations, and there was little trace of her flower garden except a single faded sprig of much-enduring French pinks, which a great bee and a yellow butterfly were befriending together. I drank at the spring, and thought that now and then some one would follow me from the busy, hard-worked, and simple-thoughted countryside of the mainland, which lay dim and dreamlike in the August haze, as Joanna must have watched it many a day. There was the world, and here was she with eternity well begun. In the life of each of us, I said to myself, there is a place remote and islanded, and given to endless regret or secret happiness; we are each the uncompanioned hermit and recluse of an hour or a day; we understand our fellows of the cell to whatever age of history they may belong.

But as I stood alone on the island, in the sea-breeze, suddenly there came a sound of distant voices; gay voices and laughter from a pleasure-boat that was going seaward full of boys and girls. I knew, as if she had told me, that poor Joanna must have heard the like on many and many a summer afternoon, and must have welcomed the good cheer in spite of hopelessness and winter weather, and all the sorrow and disappointment in the world.

XVI

The Great Expedition

MRS. TODD never by any chance gave warning over night of her great projects and adventures by sea and land. She first came to an understanding with the primal forces of nature, and never trusted to any preliminary promise of good weather, but examined the day for herself in its infancy. Then, if the stars were propitious, and the wind blew from a quarter of good inheritance whence no surprises of sea-turns or southwest sultriness might be feared, long before I was fairly awake I used to hear a rustle and knocking like a great mouse in the walls, and an impatient tread on the steep garret stairs that led to Mrs. Todd's chief place of storage. She went and came as if she had already started on her expedition with utmost haste and kept returning for something that was forgotten. When I appeared in quest of my breakfast, she would be absent-minded and sparing of speech, as if I had displeased her, and she was now, by main force of principle, holding herself back from altercation and strife of tongues.

These signs of a change became familiar to me in the course of time, and Mrs. Todd hardly noticed some plain proofs of divination one August morning when I said, without preface, that I had just seen the Beggs' best chaise go by, and that we should have to take the grocery. Mrs. Todd was alert in a moment.

"There! I might have known!" she exclaimed. "It's the 15th of August, when he goes and gets his money. He heired an annuity from an uncle o' his on his mother's side. I understood the uncle said none o' Sam Begg's wife's folks should make free with it, so after Sam's gone it'll all be past an' spent, like last summer. That's what Sam prospers on now, if you can call it prosperin'. Yes, I might have known. 'Tis the 15th o' August with him, an' he gener'ly stops to dinner with a cousin's widow on the way home. Feb'uary n' August is the times. Takes him 'bout all day to go an' come."

I heard this explanation with interest. The tone of Mrs. Todd's voice was complaining at the last.

"I like the grocery just as well as the chaise," I hastened to say, referring to a long-bodied high wagon with a canopy-top, like an attenuated four-posted bedstead on wheels, in which we sometimes journeyed. "We can put things in behind — roots and flowers and raspberries, or anything you are going after — much better than if we had the chaise."

Mrs. Todd looked stony and unwilling. "I counted upon the chaise," she said, turning her back to me, and roughly pushing back all the quiet tumblers on the cupboard shelf as if they had been impertinent. "Yes, I desired the chaise for once. I ain't goin' berryin' nor to fetch home no more wilted vegetation this year. Season's about past, except for a poor few o' late things," she added in a milder tone. "I'm goin' up country. No, I ain't intendin' to go berryin'. I've been plottin' for it the past fortnight and hopin' for a good day."

"Would you like to have me go too?" I asked frankly, but not without a humble fear that I might have mistaken the purpose of this latest plan.

"Oh certain, dear!" answered my friend affectionately. "Oh no, I never thought o' any one else for comp'ny, if it's convenient for you, long's poor mother ain't come. I ain't nothin' like so handy with a conveyance as I be with a good bo't. Comes o' my early bringing-up. I expect we've got to make that great high wagon do. The tires want settin' and 'tis all loose-jointed, so I can hear it shackle the other side o' the ridge. We'll put the basket in front. I ain't goin' to have it bouncin' an' twirlin' all the way. Why, I've been makin' some nice hearts and rounds to carry."

These were signs of high festivity, and my interest deepened moment by moment.

"I'll go down to the Beggs' and get the horse just as soon as I finish my breakfast," said I. "Then we can start whenever you are ready."

Mrs. Todd looked cloudy again. "I don't know but you look nice enough to go just as you be," she suggested doubtfully. "No, you wouldn't want to wear that pretty blue dress o' yourn 'way up country. 'Taint dusty now, but it may be comin' home. No, I expect you'd rather not wear that and the other hat."

"Oh yes. I shouldn't think of wearing these clothes," said I, with sudden illumination. "Why, if we're going up country and are likely to see some of your friends, I'll put on my blue dress, and you must wear your watch; I am not going at all if you mean to wear the big hat."

"Now you're behavin' pretty," responded Mrs. Todd, with a gay toss of her head and a cheerful smile, as she came across the room, bringing a saucerful of wild raspberries, a pretty piece of salvage from supper-time. "I was cast down when I see you come to breakfast. I didn't think 'twas just what you'd select to wear to the reunion, where you're goin' to meet everybody."

"What reunion do you mean?" I asked, not without amazement. "Not the Bowden Family's? I thought that was going to take place in September."

"To-day's the day. They sent word the middle o' the week. I thought you might have heard of it. Yes, they changed the day. I been thinkin' we'd talk it over, but you never can tell beforehand how it's goin' to be, and 'taint worth while to wear a day all out before it comes." Mrs. Todd gave no place to the pleasures of anticipation, but she spoke like the oracle that she was. "I wish mother was here to go," she continued sadly. "I did look for her last night, and I couldn't keep back the tears when the dark really fell and she wa'n't here, she does so enjoy a great occasion. If

William had a mite o' snap an' ambition, he 'd take the lead at such a time. Mother likes variety, and there ain't but a few nice opportunities 'round here, an' them she has to miss 'less she contrives to get ashore to me. I do re'lly hate to go to the reunion without mother, an' 'tis a beautiful day; everybody'll be asking where she is. Once she'd have got here anyway. Poor mother's beginnin' to feel her age."

"Why, there's your mother now!" I exclaimed with joy, I was so glad to see the dear old soul again. "I hear her voice at the gate." But Mrs. Todd was out of the door before me.

There, sure enough, stood Mrs. Blackett, who must have left Green Island before daylight. She had climbed the steep road from the waterside so eagerly that she was out of breath, and was standing by the garden fence to rest. She held an old-fashioned brown wicker cap-basket in her hand, as if visiting were a thing of every day, and looked up at us as pleased and triumphant as a child.

"Oh, what a poor, plain garden! Hardly a flower in it except your bush o' balm!" she said. "But you do keep your garden neat, Almiry. Are you both well, an' goin' up country with me?" She came a step or two closer to meet us, with quaint politeness and quite as delightful as if she were at home. She dropped a quick little curtsey before Mrs. Todd.

"There, mother, what a girl you be! I am so pleased! I was just bewailin' you," said the daughter, with unwonted feeling. "I was just bewailin' you, I was so disappointed, an' I kep' myself awake a good piece o' the night scoldin' poor William. I watched for the boat till I was ready to shed tears yesterday, and when 'twas comin' dark I kep' making errands out to the gate an' down the road to see if you wa'n't in the doldrums somewhere down the bay."

"There was a head wind, as you know," said Mrs. Blackett, giving me the cap-basket, and holding my hand affectionately as we walked up the clean-swept path to the door. "I was partly ready to come, but dear William said I should be all tired out and might get cold, havin' to beat all the way in. So we give it up, and set down and spent the evenin' together. It was a little rough and windy outside, and I guess 'twas better judgment; we went to bed very early and made a good start just at daylight. It's been a lovely mornin' on the water. William thought he'd better fetch across beyond Bird Rocks, rowin' the greater part o' the way; then we sailed from there right over to the landin', makin' only one tack. William'll be in again for me to-morrow, so I can come back here an' rest me over night, an' go to meetin' to-morrow, and have a nice, good visit."

"She was just havin' her breakfast," said Mrs. Todd, who had listened eagerly to the long explanation without a word of disapproval, while her face shone more and more with joy. "You just sit right down an' have a cup of tea and rest you while we make our preparations. Oh, I am so gratified to think you've come! Yes, she was just havin' her breakfast, and we were speakin' of you. Where's William?"

"He went right back; said he expected some schooners in about noon after bait, but he'll come an' have his dinner with us tomorrow, unless it rains; then next day. I laid his best things out all ready," explained Mrs. Blackett, a little anxiously. "This wind will serve him nice all the way home. Yes, I will take a cup of tea, dear, — a cup of tea is always good; and then I'll rest a minute and be all ready to start."

"I do feel condemned for havin' such hard thoughts o' William," openly confessed Mrs. Todd. She stood before us so large and serious that we both laughed and could not find it in our hearts to convict so rueful a culprit. "He shall have a good dinner to-morrow, if it can be got, and I shall be real glad to see William," the confession ended handsomely, while Mrs. Blackett smiled approval and made haste to praise the tea. Then I hurried away to make sure of the grocery wagon. Whatever might be the good of the reunion, I was going to have the pleasure and delight of a day in Mrs. Blackett's company, not to speak of Mrs. Todd's.

The early morning breeze was still blowing, and the warm, sunshiny air was of some ethereal northern sort, with a cool freshness as it came over new-fallen snow. The world was filled with a fragrance of fir-balsam and the faintest flavor of seaweed from the ledges, bare and brown at low tide in the little harbor. It was so still and so early that the village was but half awake. I could hear no voices but those of the birds, small and great, — the constant song sparrows, the clink of a yellow-hammer over in the woods, and the far conversation of some deliberate crows. I saw William Blackett's escaping sail already far from land, and Captain Littlepage was sitting behind his closed window as I passed by, watching for some one who never came. I tried to speak to him, but he did not see me. There was a patient look on the old man's face, as if the world were a great mistake and he had nobody with whom to speak his own language or find companionship.

XVII

A Country Road

WHATEVER DOUBTS and anxieties I may have had about the inconvenience of the Begg's high wagon for a person of Mrs. Blackett's age and shortness, they were happily overcome by the aid of a chair and her own valiant spirit. Mrs. Todd bestowed great care upon seating us as if we were taking passage by boat, but she finally pronounced that we were properly trimmed. When we had gone only a little way up the hill she remembered that she had left the house door wide open, though the large key was safe in her pocket. I offered to run back, but my offer was met with lofty scorn, and we lightly dismissed the matter from our minds, until two or three miles further on we met the doctor, and Mrs. Todd asked him to stop and ask her nearest neighbor to step over and close the door if the dust seemed to blow in the afternoon.

"She'll be there in her kitchen; she'll hear you the minute you call; 'twont give you no delay," said Mrs. Todd to the doctor. "Yes, Mis' Dennett's right there, with the windows all open. It isn't as if my fore door opened right on the road, anyway." At which proof of composure Mrs. Blackett smiled wisely at me.

The doctor seemed delighted to see our guest; they were evidently the warmest friends, and I saw a look of affectionate confidence in their eyes. The good man left his carriage to speak to us, but as he took Mrs. Blackett's hand he held it a moment, and, as if merely from force of habit, felt her pulse as they talked; then to my delight he gave the firm old wrist a commending pat.

"You're wearing well; good for another ten years at this rate," he assured her cheerfully, and she smiled back. "I like to keep a strict account of my old stand-bys," and he turned to me. "Don't you let Mrs. Todd overdo to-day, — old folks like her are apt to be thoughtless;" and then we all laughed, and, parting, went our ways gayly.

"I suppose he puts up with your rivalry the same as ever?" asked Mrs. Blackett. "You and he are as friendly as ever, I see, Almiry," and Almira sagely nodded.

"He's got too many long routes now to stop to 'tend to all his door patients," she said, "especially them that takes pleasure in talkin' themselves over. The doctor and me have got to be kind of partners; he's gone a good deal, far an' wide. Looked tired, didn't he? I shall have to advise with him an' get him off for a good rest. He'll take the big boat from Rockland an' go off up to Boston an' mouse round among the other doctors, one in two or three years, and come home fresh as a boy. I guess they think consider'ble of him up there." Mrs. Todd shook the reins and reached determinedly for the whip, as if she were compelling public opinion.

Whatever energy and spirit the white horse had to begin with were soon exhausted by the steep hills and his discernment of a long expedition ahead. We toiled slowly along. Mrs. Blackett and I sat together, and Mrs. Todd sat alone in front with much majesty and the large basket of provisions. Part of the way the road was shaded by thick woods, but we also passed one farmhouse after another on the high uplands, which we all three regarded with deep interest, the house itself and the barns and garden-spots and poultry all having to suffer an inspection of the shrewdest sort. This was a highway quite new to me; in fact, most of my journeys with Mrs. Todd had been made afoot and between the roads, in open pasturelands. My friends stopped several times for brief dooryard visits, and made so many promises of stopping again on the way home that I began to wonder how long the expedition would last. I had often noticed how warmly Mrs. Todd was greeted by her friends, but it was hardly to be compared with the feeling now shown toward Mrs. Blackett. A look of delight came to the faces of those who recognized the plain, dear old figure beside me; one revelation after another was made of the constant interest and intercourse that had linked the far island and these scattered farms into a golden chain of love and dependence.

"Now, we musn't stop again if we can help it," insisted Mrs. Todd at last. "You'll get tired, mother, and you'll think the less o' reunions. We can visit along here any day. There, if they ain't frying doughnuts in this next house, too! These are new folks, you know, from over St. George way; they took this old Talcot farm last year. 'Tis the best water on the road, and the check-rein's come undone — yes, we'd best delay a little and water the horse."

We stopped, and seeing a party of pleasure-seekers in holiday attire, the thin, anxious mistress of the farmhouse came out with wistful sympathy to hear what news we might have to give. Mrs. Blackett first spied her at the half-closed door, and asked with such cheerful directness if we were trespassing that, after a few words, she went back to her kitchen and reappeared with a plateful of doughnuts.

"Entertainment for man and beast," announced Mrs. Todd with

satisfaction. "Why, we've perceived there was new doughnuts all along the road, but you're the first that has treated us."

Our new acquaintance flushed with pleasure, but said nothing.

"They're very nice; you've had good luck with 'em," pronounced Mrs. Todd. "Yes, we've observed there was doughnuts all the way along; if one house is frying all the rest is; 'tis so with a great many things."

"I don't suppose likely you're goin' up to the Bowden reunion?" asked the hostess as the white horse lifted his head and we were saying good-by.

"Why, yes," said Mrs. Blackett and Mrs. Todd and I, all together.

"I am connected with the family. Yes, I expect to be there this afternoon. I've been lookin' forward to it," she told us eagerly.

"We shall see you there. Come and sit with us if it's convenient," said dear Mrs. Blackett, and we drove away.

"I wonder who she was before she was married?" said Mrs. Todd, who was usually unerring in matters of genealogy. "She must have been one of that remote branch that lived down beyond Thomaston. We can find out this afternoon. I expect that the families'll march together, or be sorted out some way. I'm willing to own a relation that has such proper ideas of doughnuts."

"I seem to see the family looks," said Mrs. Blackett. "I wish we'd asked her name. She's a stranger, and I want to help make it pleasant for all such."

"She resembles Cousin Pa'lina Bowden about the forehead," said Mrs. Todd with decision.

We had just passed a piece of woodland that shaded the road, and come out to some open fields beyond, when Mrs. Todd suddenly reined in the horse as if somebody had stood on the roadside and stopped her. She even gave that quick reassuring nod of her head which was usually made to answer for a bow, but I discovered that she was looking eagerly at a tall ash-tree that grew just inside the field fence.

"I thought 'twas goin' to do well," she said complacently as we went on again. "Last time I was up this way that tree was kind of drooping and discouraged. Grown trees act that way sometimes, same's folks; then they'll put right to it and strike their roots off into new ground and start all over again with real good courage. Ash-trees is very likely to have poor spells; they ain't got the resolution of other trees."

I listened hopefully for more; it was this peculiar wisdom that made one value Mrs. Todd's pleasant company.

"There's sometimes a good hearty tree growin' right out of the bare rock, out o' some crack that just holds the roots;" she went on to say, "right on the pitch o' one o' them bare stony hills where you can't seem to see a wheel-barrowful o' good earth in a place, but that tree'll keep a green top in the driest summer. You lay your ear down to the ground an' you'll hear a little stream runnin'. Every such tree has got its own livin' spring; there's folk made to match 'em."

I could not help turning to look at Mrs. Blackett, close beside me. Her hands were clasped placidly in their thin black woolen gloves, and she was looking at the flowery wayside as we went slowly along, with a pleased, expectant smile. I do not think she had heard a word about the trees.

"I just saw a nice plant o' elecampane growin' back there," she said presently to her daughter.

"I haven't got my mind on herbs to-day," responded Mrs. Todd, in the most matter-of-fact way. "I'm bent on seeing folks," and she shook the reins again.

I for one had no wish to hurry, it was so pleasant in the shady roads. The woods stood close to the road on the right; on the left were narrow fields and pastures where there were as many acres of spruces and pines as there were acres of bay and juniper and huckleberry, with a little turf between. When I thought we were in the heart of the inland country, we reached the top of a hill, and suddenly there lay spread out before us a wonderful great view of well-cleared fields that swept down to the wide water of a bay. Beyond this were distant shores like another country in the midday haze which half hid the hills beyond, and the faraway pale blue mountains on the northern horizon. There was a schooner with all sails set coming down the bay from a white village that was sprinkled on the shore, and there were many sailboats flitting about. It was a noble landscape, and my eyes, which had grown used to the narrow inspection of a shaded roadside, could hardly take it in.

"Why, it's the upper bay," said Mrs. Todd. "You can see 'way over into the town of Fessenden. Those farms 'way over there are all in Fessenden. Mother used to have a sister that lived up that shore. If we started as early's we could on a summer mornin', we couldn't get to her place from Green Island till late afternoon, even with a fair, steady breeze, and you had to strike the time just right so as to fetch up 'long o' the tide and land near the flood. 'Twas ticklish business, an' we didn't visit back an' forth as much as mother desired. You have to go 'way down the co'st to Cold Spring Light an' round that long point, — up here's what they call the Back Shore."

"No, we were 'most always separated, my dear sister and me, after the first year she was married," said Mrs. Blackett. "We had our little families an' plenty o' cares. We were always lookin' forward to the time we could see each other more. Now and then she'd get out to the island for a few days while her husband'd go fishin'; and once he stopped with her an' two children, and made him some flakes right there and cured all his fish for winter. We did have a beautiful time together, sister an' me; she used to look back to it long's she lived.

"I do love to look over there where she used to live," Mrs. Blackett went on as we began to go down the hill. "It seems as if she must still be there, though she's long been gone. She loved their farm, — she didn't see how I got so used to our island; but somehow I was always happy from the first."

"Yes, it's very dull to me up among those slow farms," declared Mrs. Todd. "The snow troubles 'em in winter. They're all besieged by winter, as you may say; 'tis far better by the shore than up among such places. I never thought I should like to live up country."

"Why, just see the carriages ahead of us on the next rise!" exclaimed Mrs. Blackett. "There's going to be a great gathering, don't you believe there is, Almiry? It hasn't seemed up to now as if anybody was going but us. An' 'tis such a beautiful day, with yesterday cool and pleasant to work an' get ready, I shouldn't wonder if everybody was there, even the slow ones like Phebe Ann Brock."

Mrs. Blackett's eyes were bright with excitement, and even Mrs. Todd showed remarkable enthusiasm. She hurried the horse and caught up with the holiday-makers ahead. "There's all the Dep'fords goin', six in the wagon," she told us joyfully; "an' Mis' Alva Tilley's folks are now risin' the hill in their new carry-all."

Mrs. Blackett pulled at the neat bow of her black bonnet-strings, and tied them again with careful precision. "I believe your bonnet's on a little bit sideways, dear," she advised Mrs. Todd as if she were a child; but Mrs. Todd was too much occupied to pay proper heed. We began to feel a new sense of gayety and of taking part in the great occasion as we joined the little train.

XVIII

The Bowden Reunion

IT IS VERY RARE in country life, where high days and holidays are few, that any occasion of general interest proves to be less than great. Such is the hidden fire of enthusiasm in the New England nature that, once given an outlet, it shines forth with almost volcanic light and heat. In quiet neighborhoods such inward force does not waste itself upon those petty excitements of every day that belong to cities, but when, at long intervals, the altars to patriotism, to friendship, to the ties of kindred, are reared in our familiar fields, then the fires glow, the flames come up as if from the inexhaustible burning heart of the earth; the primal fires break through the granite dust in which our souls are set. Each heart is warm and every face shines with the ancient light. Such a day as this has transfiguring powers, and easily makes friends of those who have been cold-hearted, and gives to those who are dumb their chance to speak, and lends some beauty to the plainest face.

"Oh, I expect I shall meet friends today that I haven't seen in a long while," said Mrs. Blackett with deep satisfaction. " 'Twill bring out a good many of the old folks, 'tis such a lovely day. I'm always glad not to have them disappointed."

"I guess likely the best of 'em'll be there," answered Mrs. Todd with gentle humor, stealing a glance at me. "There's one thing certain: there's nothing takes in this whole neighborhood like anything related to the Bowdens. Yes, I do feel that when you call upon the Bowdens you may expect most families to rise up between the Landing and the far end of the Back Cove. Those that aren't kin by blood are kin by marriage."

"There used to be an old story goin' about when I was a girl," said Mrs. Blackett, with much amusement. "There was a great many more Bowdens then than there are now, and the folks was all setting in meeting a dreadful hot Sunday afternoon, and a scatter-witted little bound girl came running to the meetin'-house door all out o' breath from somewheres in the neighborhood. 'Mis' Bowden, Mis' Bowden!' says she. 'Your baby's in a fit!' They used to tell that the whole congregation was up on its feet in a minute and right out into the aisles. All the Mis' Bowdens was setting right out for home; the minister stood there in the pulpit tryin' to keep sober, an' all at once he burst right out laughin'. He was a very nice man, they said, and he said he'd better give 'em the benediction, and they could hear the sermon next Sunday, so he kept it over. My mother was there, and she thought certain 'twas me."

"None of our family was ever subject to fits," interrupted Mrs. Todd severely. "No, we never had fits, none of us, and 'twas lucky we didn't 'way out there to Green Island. Now these folks right in front: dear sakes knows the bunches o' soothing catnip an' yarrow I've had to favor old Mis' Evins with dryin'! You can see it right in their expressions, all them Evins folks. There, just you look up to the crossroads, mother," she suddenly exclaimed. "See all the teams ahead of us. And oh, look down on the bay; yes, look down on the bay! See what a sight o' boats, all headin' for the Bowden place cove!"

"Oh, ain't it beautiful!" said Mrs. Blackett, with all the delight of a girl. She stood up in the high wagon to see everything, and when she sat down again she took fast hold of my hand.

"Hadn't you better urge the horse a little, Almiry?" she asked. "He's had it easy as we came along, and he can rest when we get there. The others are some little ways ahead, and I don't want to lose a minute."

We watched the boats drop their sails one by one in the cove as we drove along the high land. The old Bowden house stood, low-storied and broad-roofed, in its green fields as if it were a motherly brown hen waiting for the flock that came straying toward it from every direction. The first Bowden settler had made his home there, and it was still the Bowden farm; five generations of sailors and farmers and soldiers had been its children. And presently Mrs. Blackett showed me the stone-walled burying-ground that stood like a little fort on a knoll overlooking the bay, but, as she said, there were plenty of scattered Bowdens who were not laid there, — some lost at sea, and some out West, and some who died in the war; most of the home graves were those of women.

We could see now that there were different footpaths from along shore and across country. In all these there were straggling processions walking in single file, like old illustrations of the Pilgrim's Progress. There was a crowd about the house as if huge bees were swarming in the lilac bushes. Beyond the fields and cove a higher point of land ran out into the bay, covered with woods which must have kept away much of the northwest wind in winter. Now there was a pleasant look of shade and shelter there for the great family meeting.

We hurried on our way, beginning to feel as if we were very late, and it was a great satisfaction at last to turn out of the stony highroad into a green lane shaded with old apple-trees. Mrs. Todd encouraged the horse until he fairly pranced with gayety as we drove round to the front of the house on the soft turf. There was an instant cry of rejoicing, and two or three persons ran toward us from the busy group.

"Why, dear Mis' Blackett! — here's Mis' Blackett!" I heard them say, as if it were pleasure enough for one day to have a sight of her. Mrs. Todd turned to me with a lovely look of triumph and self-forgetfulness. An elderly man who wore the look of a prosperous sea-captain put up both arms and lifted Mrs. Blackett down from the high wagon like a child, and kissed her with hearty affection. "I was master afraid she wouldn't be here," he said, looking at Mrs. Todd with a face like a happy sunburnt schoolboy, while everybody crowded round to give their welcome.

"Mother's always the queen," said Mrs. Todd. "Yes, they'll all make everything of mother; she'll have a lovely time to-day. I wouldn't have had her miss it, and there won't be a thing she'll ever regret, except to mourn because William wa'n't here."

Mrs. Blackett having been properly escorted to the house, Mrs. Todd received her own full share of honor, and some of the men, with a simple kindness that was the soul of chivalry, waited upon us and our baskets and led away the white horse. I already knew some of Mrs. Todd's friends and kindred, and felt like an adopted Bowden in this happy moment. It seemed to be enough for anyone to have arrived by the same conveyance as Mrs. Blackett, who presently had her court inside the house, while Mrs. Todd, large, hospitable, and preeminent, was the centre of a rapidly increasing crowd about the lilac bushes. Small companies were continually coming up the long green slope from the water, and nearly all the boats had come to shore. I counted three or four that were baffled by the light breeze, but before long all the Bowdens, small and great, seemed to have assembled, and we started to go up to the grove across the field.

Out of the chattering crowd of noisy children, and large-waisted women whose best black dresses fell straight to the ground in generous folds, and sunburnt men who looked as serious as if it were town-meeting day, there suddenly came silence and order. I saw the straight, soldierly little figure of a man who bore a fine resemblance to Mrs. Blackett, and who appeared to marshal us with perfect ease. He was imperative enough, but with a grand military sort of courtesy, and bore himself with solemn dignity of importance. We were sorted out according to some clear design of his own, and stood as speechless as a troop to await his orders. Even the children were ready to march together, a pretty flock, and at the last moment Mrs. Blackett and a few distinguished companions, the ministers and those who were very old, came out of the house together and took their places. We ranked by fours, and even then we made a long procession.

There was a wide path mowed for us across the field, and, as we moved along, the birds flew up out of the thick second crop of clover, and the bees hummed as if it still were June. There was a flashing of white gulls over the water where the fleet of boats rode the low waves together in the cove, swaying their small masts as if they kept time to our steps. The plash of the water could be heard faintly, yet still be heard; we might have been a company of ancient Greeks going to celebrate a victory, or to worship the god of harvests, in the grove above. It was strangely moving to see this and to make part of it. The sky, the sea, have watched poor humanity at its rites so long; we were no more a New England family celebrating its own existence and simple progress; we carried the tokens and inheritance of all such households from which this had descended, and were only the latest of our line. We possessed the instincts of a far, forgotten childhood; I found myself thinking that we ought to be carrying green branches and singing as we went. So we came to the thick shaded grove still silent, and were set in our places by the straight trees that swayed together and let sunshine through here and there like a single golden leaf that flickered down, vanishing in the cool shade.

The grove was so large that the great family looked far smaller than it had in the open field; there was a thick growth of dark pines and firs with an occasional maple or oak that gave a gleam of color like a bright window in the great roof. On three sides we could see the water, shining behind the tree-trunks, and feel the cool salt breeze that began to come up with the tide just as the day reached its highest point of heat. We could see the green sunlit field we had just crossed as if we looked out at it from a dark room, and the old house and its lilacs standing placidly in the sun, and the great barn with a stockade of carriages from which two or three care-taking men who had lingered were coming across the field together. Mrs. Todd had taken off her warm gloves and looked the picture of content.

"There!" she exclaimed. "I've always meant to have you see this place, but I never looked for such a beautiful opportunity — weather an' occasion both made to match. Yes, it suits me: I don't ask no more. I want to know if you saw mother walkin' at the head! It choked me right up to see mother at the head, walkin' with the ministers," and Mrs. Todd turned away to hide the feelings she could not instantly control.

"Who was the marshal?" I hastened to ask. "Was he an old soldier?"

"Don't he do well?" answered Mrs. Todd with satisfaction.

"He don't often have such a chance to show off his gifts," said Mrs. Caplin, a friend from the Landing who had joined us. "That's Sant Bowden; he always takes the lead, such days. Good for nothing else most o' his time; trouble is, he" —

I turned with interest to hear the worst. Mrs. Caplin's tone was both zealous and impressive.

"Stim'lates," she explained scornfully.

"No, Santin never was in the war," said Mrs. Todd with lofty indifference. "It was a cause of real distress to him. He kep' enlistin', and traveled far an' wide about here, an' even took the bo't and went to Boston to volunteer; but he ain't a sound man, an' they wouldn't have him. They say he knows all their tactics, an' can tell all about the battle o' Waterloo well's he can Bunker Hill. I told him once the country'd lost a great general, an' I meant it, too."

"I expect you're near right," said Mrs. Caplin, a little crestfallen and apologetic.

"I be right," insisted Mrs. Todd with much amiability. " 'Twas most too bad to cramp him down to his peaceful trade, but he's a most excellent shoemaker at his best, an' he always says it's a trade that gives him time to think an' plan his maneuvers. Over to the Port they always invite him to march Decoration Day, same as the rest, an' he does look noble; he comes of soldier stock."

I had been noticing with great interest the curiously French type of face which prevailed in this rustic company. I had said to myself before that Mrs. Blackett was plainly of French descent, in both her appearance and her charming gifts, but this is not surprising when one has learned how large a proportion of the early settlers on this northern coast of New England were of Huguenot blood, and that it is the Norman Englishman, not the Saxon, who goes adventuring to a new world.

"They used to say in old times," said Mrs. Todd modestly, "that our family came of very high folks in France, and one of 'em was a great general in some o' the old wars. I sometimes think that Santin's ability has come 'way down from then. 'Tain't nothin' he's ever acquired; 'twas born in him. I don't know's he ever saw a fine parade, or met with those that studied up such things. He's figured it all out an' got his papers so he knows how to aim a cannon right for William's fish-house five miles out on Green Island, or up there on Burnt Island where the signal is. He had it all over to me one day, an' I tried hard to appear interested. His life's all in it, but he will have those poor gloomy spells come over him now an' then, an' then he has to drink."

Mrs. Caplin gave a heavy sigh.

"There's a great many such strayaway folks, just as there is plants," continued Mrs. Todd, who was nothing if not botanical. "I know of just one sprig of laurel that grows over back here in a wild spot, an' I never could hear of no other on this coast. I had a large bunch brought me once from Massachusetts way, so I know it. This piece grows in an open spot where you'd think 'twould do well, but it's sort o' poor-lookin'. I've visited it time an' again, just to notice its poor blooms. 'Tis a real Sant Bowden, out of its own place."

Mrs. Caplin looked bewildered and blank. "Well, all I know is, last year he worked out some kind of plan so's to parade the county conference in platoons, and got 'em all flustered up tryin' to sense his ideas of a holler square," she burst forth. "They was holler enough anyway after ridin' 'way down from up country into the salt air, and they'd been treated to a sermon on faith an' works from old Faythter Harlow that never knows when to cease. 'Twa'n't no time for tactics then, — they wa'n't a-thinkin' of the church military. Sant, he couldn't do nothin' with 'em. All he thinks of, when he sees a crowd, is how to march 'em. 'Tis all very well when he don't 'tempt too much. He never did act like other folks."

"Ain't I just been maintainin' that he ain't like 'em?" urged Mrs. Todd decidedly. "Strange folks has got to have strange ways, for what I see."

"Somebody observed once that you could pick out the likeness of 'most every sort of a foreigner when you looked about you in our parish," said Sister Caplin, her face brightening with sudden illumination. "I didn't see the bearin' of it then quite so plain. I always did think Mari' Harris resembled a Chinee."

"Mari' Harris was pretty as a child, I remember," said the pleasant voice of Mrs. Blackett, who, after receiving the affectionate greetings of nearly the whole company, came to join us, — to see, as she insisted, that we were out of mischief.

"Yes, Mari' was one o' them pretty little lambs that make dreadful homely old sheep," replied Mrs. Todd with energy. "Cap'n Littlepage never'd look so disconsolate if she was any sort of a proper person to direct things. She might divert him; yes, she might divert the old gentleman, an' let him think he had his own way, 'stead o' arguing everything down to the bare bone. 'Twouldn't hurt her to sit down an' hear his great stories once in a while."

"The stories are very interesting," I ventured to say.

"Yes, you always catch yourself a-thinkin' what if they was all true, and he had the right of it," answered Mrs. Todd. "He's a good sight better company, though dreamy, than such sordid creatur's as Mari' Harris."

"Live and let live," said dear old Mrs. Blackett gently. "I haven't seen the captain for a good while, now that I ain't so constant to meetin'," she added wistfully. "We always have known each other."

"Why, if it is a good pleasant day tomorrow, I'll get William to call an' invite the capt'in to dinner. William'll be in early so's to pass up the street without meetin' anybody."

"There, they're callin' out it's time to set the tables," said Mrs. Caplin, with great excitement.

"Here's Cousin Sarah Jane Blackett! Well, I am pleased, certain!" exclaimed Mrs. Todd, with unaffected delight; and these kindred spirits met and parted with the promise of a good talk later on. After this there was no more time for conversation until we were seated in order at the long tables.

"I'm one that always dreads seeing some o' the folks that I don't like, at such a time as this," announced Mrs. Todd privately to me after a season of reflection. We were just waiting for the feast to begin. "You wouldn't think such a great creatur' 's I be could feel all over pins an' needles. I remember, the day I promised to Nathan, how it come over me, just's I was feelin' happy's I could, that I'd got to have an own cousin o' his for my near relation all the rest o' my life, an' it seemed as if die I should. Poor Nathan saw somethin' had crossed me, — he had very nice feelings, — and when he asked what 'twas, I told him. 'I never could like her myself,' said he. 'You sha'n't be bothered, dear,' he says; an' 'twas one o' the things that made me set a good deal by Nathan, he did not make a habit of always opposin', like some men. 'Yes,' says I, 'but think o' Thanksgivin' times an' funerals; she's our relation, an' we've got to own her.' Young folks don't think o' those things. There she goes now, do let's pray her by!" said Mrs. Todd, with an alarming transition from general opinions to particular animosities. "I hate her just the same as I always did; but she's got on a real pretty dress. I do try to remember that she's Nathan's cousin. Oh dear, well; she's gone by after all, an' ain't seen me. I expected she'd come pleasantin' round just to show off an' say afterwards she was acquainted."

This was so different from Mrs. Todd's usual largeness of mind that I had a moment's uneasiness; but the cloud passed quickly over her spirit, and was gone with the offender.

There never was a more generous out-of-door feast along the coast than the Bowden family set forth that day. To call it a picnic would make it seem trivial. The great tables were edged with pretty oak-leaf trimming, which the boys and girls made. We brought flowers from the fence-thickets of the great field; and out of the disorder of flowers and provisions suddenly appeared as orderly a scheme for the feast as the marshal had shaped for the procession. I began to respect the Bowdens for their inheritance of good taste and skill and a certain pleasing gift of formality. Something made them do all these things in a finer way than most country people would have done them. As I looked up and down the tables there was a good cheer, a grave soberness that shone with pleasure, a humble dignity of bearing. There were some who should have sat below the salt for lack of this good breeding; but they were not many. So, I said to myself, their ancestors may have sat in the great hall of some old French house in the Middle Ages, when battles and sieges and processions and feasts were familiar things. The ministers and Mrs.

Blackett, with a few of their rank and age, were put in places of honor, and for once that I looked any other way I looked twice at Mrs. Blackett's face, serene and mindful of privilege and responsibility, the mistress by simple fitness of this great day.

Mrs. Todd looked up at the roof of green trees, and then carefully surveyed the company. "I see 'em better now they're all settin' down," she said with satisfaction. "There's old Mr. Gilbraith and his sister. I wish they were sittin' with us; they're not among folks they can parley with, an' they look disappointed."

As the feast went on, the spirits of my companion steadily rose. The excitement of an unexpectedly great occasion was a subtle stimulant to her disposition, and I could see that sometimes when Mrs. Todd had seemed limited and heavily domestic, she had simply grown sluggish for lack of proper surroundings. She was not so much reminiscent now as expectant, and as alert and gay as a girl. We who were her neighbors were full of gayety, which was but the reflected light from her beaming countenance. It was not the first time that I was full of wonder at the waste of human ability in this world, as a botanist wonders at the wastefulness of nature, the thousand seeds that die, the unused provision of every sort. The reserve force of society grows more and more amazing to one's thought. More than one face among the Bowdens showed that only opportunity and stimulus were lacking, — a narrow set of circumstances had caged a fine able character and held it captive. One sees exactly the same types in a country gathering as in the most brilliant city company. You are safe to be understood if the spirit of your speech is the same for one neighbor as for the other.

XIX

The Feast's End

THE FEAST WAS a noble feast, as has already been said. There was an elegant ingenuity displayed in the form of pies which delighted my heart. Once acknowledge that an American pie is far to be preferred to its humble ancestor, the English tart, and it is joyful to be reassured at a Bowden reunion that invention has not yet failed. Beside a delightful variety of material, the decorations went beyond all my former experience; dates and names were wrought in lines of pastry and frosting on the tops. There was even more elaborate reading matter on an excellent early-apple pie which we began to share and eat, precept upon precept. Mrs. Todd helped me generously to the whole word *Bowden*, and consumed *Reunion* herself, save an undecipherable fragment; but the most renowned essay in cookery on the tables was a model of the old Bowden house made of durable gingerbread, with all the windows and doors in the right places, and sprigs of genuine lilac set at the front. It must have been baked in sections, in one of the last of the great brick ovens, and fastened together on the morning of the day. There was a general sigh when this fell into ruin at the feast's end, and it was shared by a great part of the assembly, not without seriousness, and as if it were a pledge and token of loyalty. I met the maker of the gingerbread house, which had called up lively remembrances of a childish story. She had the gleaming eye of an enthusiast and a look of high ideals.

"I could just as well have made it all of frosted cake," she said, "but 'twouldn't have been the right shade; the old house, as you observe, was never painted, and I concluded that plain gingerbread would represent it best. It wasn't all I expected it would be," she said sadly, as many an artist had said before her of his work.

There were speeches by the ministers; and there proved to be a historian among the Bowdens, who gave some fine anecdotes of the family history; and then appeared a poetess, whom Mrs. Todd regarded with wistful compassion and indulgence, and when the long faded garland of verses came to an appealing end, she turned to me with words of praise.

"Sounded pretty," said the generous listener. "Yes, I thought she did very well. We went to school together, an' Mary Anna had a very hard time; trouble was, her mother thought she'd given birth to a genius, an' Mary Anna's come to believe it herself. There, I don't know what we should have done without her; there ain't nobody else that can write poetry between here and 'way up towards Rockland; it adds a great deal at such a time. When she speaks o' those that are gone, she feels it all, and so does everybody else, but she harps too much. I'd laid half of that away for next time, if I was Mary Anna. There comes mother to speak to her, an' old Mr. Gilbraith's sister; now she'll be heartened right up. Mother'll say just the right thing."

The leave-takings were as affecting as the meetings of these old friends had been. There were enough young persons at the reunion, but it is the old who really value such opportunities; as for the young, it is the habit of every day to meet their comrades, — the time of separation has

not come. To see the joy with which these elder kinsfolk and acquaintances had looked in one another's faces, and the lingering touch of
their friendly hands; to see these affectionate meetings and then the
reluctant partings, gave one a new idea of the isolation in which it was
possible to live in that after all thinly settled region. They did not expect
to see one another again very soon; the steady, hard work on the farms,
the difficulty of getting from place to place, especially in winter when
boats were laid up, gave double value to any occasion which could bring
a large number of families together. Even funerals in this country of the
pointed firs were not without their social advantages and satisfactions. I
heard the words "next summer" repeated many times, though summer
was still ours and all the leaves were green.

The boats began to put out from shore, and the wagons to drive away.
Mrs. Blackett took me into the old house when we came back from the
grove: it was her father's birthplace and early home, and she had spent
much of her own childhood there with her grandmother. She spoke of
those days as if they had but lately passed; in fact, I could imagine that
the house looked almost exactly the same to her. I could see the brown
rafters of the unfinished roof as I looked up the steep staircase, though
the best room was as handsome with its good wainscoting and touch of
ornament on the cornice as any old room of its day in a town.

Some of the guests who came from a distance were still sitting in the
best room when we went in to take leave of the master and mistress of
the house. We all said eagerly what a pleasant day it had been, and how
swiftly the time had passed. Perhaps it is the great national anniversaries
which our country has lately kept, and the soldiers' meetings that take
place everywhere, which have made reunions of every sort the fashion.
This one, at least, had been very interesting. I fancied that old feuds had
been overlooked, and the old saying that blood is thicker than water had
again proved itself true, though from the variety of names one argued a
certain adulteration of the Bowden traits and belongings. Clannishness
is an instinct of the heart, — it is more than a birthright, or a custom; and
lesser rights were forgotten in the claim to a common inheritance.

We were among the very last to return to our proper lives and
lodgings. I came near to feeling like a true Bowden, and parted from
certain new friends as if they were old friends; we were rich with the
treasure of a new remembrance.

At last we were in the high wagon again; the old white horse had been
well fed in the Bowden barn, and we drove away and soon began to
climb the long hill toward the wooded ridge. The road was new to me, as
roads always are, going back. Most of our companions had been full of

anxious thoughts of home, — of the cows, or of young children likely to fall into disaster, — but we had no reasons for haste, and drove slowly along, talking and resting by the way. Mrs. Todd said once that she really hoped her front door had been shut on account of the dust blowing in, but added that nothing made any weight on her mind except not to forget to turn a few late mullein leaves that were drying on a newspaper in the little loft. Mrs. Blackett and I gave our word of honor that we would remind her of this heavy responsibility. The way seemed short, we had so much to talk about. We climbed hills where we could see the great bay and the islands, and then went down into shady valleys where the air began to feel like evening, cool and damp with a fragrance of wet ferns. Mrs. Todd alighted once or twice, refusing all assistance in securing some boughs of a rare shrub which she valued for its bark, though she proved incommunicative as to her reasons. We passed the house where we had been so kindly entertained with doughnuts earlier in the day, and found it closed and deserted, which was a disappointment.

"They must have stopped to tea somewheres and thought they'd finish up the day," said Mrs. Todd. "Those that enjoyed it best'll want to get right home so's to think it over."

"I didn't see the woman there after all, did you?" asked Mrs. Blackett as the horse stopped to drink at the trough.

"Oh yes, I spoke with her," answered Mrs. Todd, with but scant interest or approval. "She ain't a member o' our family."

"I thought you said she resembled Cousin Pa'lina Bowden about the forehead," suggested Mrs. Blackett.

"Well, she don't," answered Mrs. Todd impatiently. "I ain't one that's ord'narily mistaken about family likenesses, and she didn't seem to meet with friends, so I went square up to her. 'I expect you're a Bowden by your looks,' says I. 'Yes, I can take it you're one o' the Bowdens.' 'Lor', no,' says she. 'Dennett was my maiden name, but I married a Bowden for my first husband. I thought I'd come an' just see what was a-goin' on'!"

Mrs. Blackett laughed heartily. "I'm goin' to remember to tell William o' that," she said. "There, Almiry, the only thing that's troubled me all this day is to think how William would have enjoyed it. I do so wish William had been there."

"I sort of wish he had, myself," said Mrs. Todd frankly.

"There wa'n't many old folks there, somehow," said Mrs. Blackett, with a touch of sadness in her voice. "There ain't so many to come as there used to be, I'm aware, but I expected to see more."

"I thought they turned out pretty well, when you come to think of it; why, everybody was sayin' so an' feelin' gratified," answered Mrs. Todd hastily with pleasing unconsciousness; then I saw the quick color flash into her cheek, and presently she made some excuse to turn and steal an anxious look at her mother. Mrs. Blackett was smiling and thinking about her happy day, though she began to look a little tired. Neither of my companions was troubled by her burden of years. I hoped in my heart that I might be like them as I lived on into age, and then smiled to think that I too was no longer very young. So we always keep the same hearts, though our outer framework fails and shows the touch of time.

" 'Twas pretty when they sang the hymn, wasn't it?" asked Mrs. Blackett at suppertime, with real enthusiasm. "There was such a plenty o' men's voices; where I sat it did sound beautiful. I had to stop and listen when they came to the last verse."

I saw that Mrs. Todd's broad shoulders began to shake. "There was good singers there; yes, there was excellent singers," she agreed heartily, putting down her teacup, "but I chanced to drift alongside Mis' Peter Bowden o' Great Bay, an' I couldn't help thinkin' if she was as far out o' town as she was out o' tune, she wouldn't get back in a day."

XX

Along Shore

ONE DAY as I went along the shore beyond the old wharves and the newer, high-stepped fabric of the steamer landing, I saw that all the boats were beached, and the slack water period of the early afternoon prevailed. Nothing was going on, not even the most leisurely of occupations, like baiting trawls or mending nets, or repairing lobster pots; the very boats seemed to be taking an afternoon nap in the sun. I could hardly discover a distant sail as I looked seaward, except a weather-beaten lobster smack, which seemed to have been taken for a plaything by the light airs that blew about the bay. It drifted and turned about so aimlessly in the wide reach off Burnt Island, that I suspected there was nobody at the wheel, or that she might have parted her rusty anchor chain while all the crew were asleep.

I watched her for a minute or two; she was the old Miranda, owned by some of the Caplins, and I knew her by an odd shaped patch of newish duck that was set into the peak of her dingy mainsail. Her vagaries offered such an exciting subject for conversation that my heart rejoiced at the sound of a hoarse voice behind me. At that moment, before I had time to answer, I saw something large and shapeless flung from the Miranda's deck that splashed the water high against her black side, and my companion gave a satisfied chuckle. The old lobster smack's sail caught the breeze again at this moment, and she moved off down the bay. Turning, I found old Elijah Tilley, who had come softly out of his dark fish-house, as if it were a burrow.

"Boy got kind o' drowsy steerin' of her; Monroe he hove him right overboard; 'wake now fast enough," explained Mr. Tilley, and we laughed together.

I was delighted, for my part, that the vicissitudes and dangers of the Miranda, in a rocky channel, should have given me this opportunity to make acquaintance with an old fisherman to whom I had never spoken. At first he had seemed to be one of those evasive and uncomfortable persons who are so suspicious of you that they make you almost suspicious of yourself. Mr. Elijah Tilley appeared to regard a stranger with scornful indifference. You might see him standing on the pebble beach or in a fish-house doorway, but when you came nearer he was gone. He was one of the small company of elderly, gaunt-shaped great fisherman whom I used to like to see leading up a deep-laden boat by the head, as if it were a horse, from the water's edge to the steep slope of the pebble beach. There were four of these large old men at the Landing, who were the survivors of an earlier and more vigorous generation. There was an alliance and understanding between them, so close that it was apparently speechless. They gave much time to watching one another's boats go out or come in; they lent a ready hand at tending one another's lobster traps in rough weather; they helped to clean the fish or to sliver porgies for the trawls, as if they were in close partnership; and when a boat came in from deep-sea fishing they were never too far out of the way, and hastened to help carry it ashore, two by two, splashing alongside, or holding its steady head, as if it were a willful sea colt. As a matter of fact no boat could help being steady and way-wise under their instant direction and companionship. Abel's boat and Jonathan Bowden's boat were as distinct and experienced personalities as the men themselves, and as inexpressive. Arguments and opinions were unknown to the conversation of these ancient friends; you would as soon have expected to hear small talk in a company of elephants as to hear old Mr. Bowden or Elijah Tilley and their two mates waste breath upon any form of trivial gossip. They made brief statements to one another from time to time. As you came to know them you wondered more and more that they should talk at all. Speech seemed to be a light and elegant accomplishment, and their unexpected acquaintance with its arts made them of new value to the listener. You felt almost as if a landmark pine should suddenly address you in regard to the weather, or a lofty-minded old camel make a remark as you stood respectfully near him under the circus tent.

I often wondered a great deal about the inner life and thought of these self-contained old fishermen; their minds seemed to be fixed upon nature and the elements rather than upon any contrivances of man, like politics or theology. My friend, Captain Bowden, who was the nephew of the eldest of this group, regarded them with deference; but he did not belong to their secret companionship, though he was neither young nor talkative.

"They've gone together ever since they were boys, they know most everything about the sea amon'st them," he told me once. "They was always just as you see 'em now since the memory of man."

These ancient seafarers had houses and lands not outwardly different from other Dunnet Landing dwellings, and two of them were fathers of families, but their true dwelling places were the sea, and the stony beach that edged its familiar shore, and the fish-houses, where much salt brine from the mackerel kits had soaked the very timbers into a state of brown permanence and petrifaction. It had also affected the old fishermen's hard complexions, until one fancied that when Death claimed them it could only be with the aid, not of any slender modern dart, but the good serviceable harpoon of a seventeenth century woodcut.

Elijah Tilley was such an evasive, discouraged-looking person, heavy-headed, and stooping so that one could never look him in the face, that even after his friendly exclamation about Monroe Pennell, the lobster smack's skipper, and the sleepy boy, I did not venture at once to speak again. Mr. Tilley was carrying a small haddock in one hand, and presently shifted it to the other hand lest it might touch my skirt. I knew that my company was accepted, and we walked together a little way.

"You mean to have a good supper," I ventured to say, by way of friendliness.

"Goin' to have this 'ere haddock an' some o' my good baked potatoes; must eat to live," responded my companion with great pleasantness and open approval. I found that I had suddenly left the forbidding coast and come into the smooth little harbor of friendship.

"You ain't never been up to my place," said the old man. "Folks don't

come now as they used to; no, 'tain't no use to ask folks now. My poor
dear she was a great hand to draw young company."

I remembered that Mrs. Todd had once said that this old fisherman
had been sore stricken and unconsoled at the death of his wife.

"I should like very much to come," said I. "Perhaps you are going to be
at home later on?"

Mr. Tilley agreed, by a sober nod, and went his way bent-shouldered
and with a rolling gait. There was a new patch high on the shoulder of
his old waistcoat, which corresponded to the renewing of the Miranda's
mainsail down the bay, and I wondered if his own fingers, clumsy with
much deep-sea fishing, had set it in.

"Was there a good catch to-day?" I asked, stopping a moment. "I
didn't happen to be on the shore when the boats came in."

"No; all come in pretty light," answered Mr. Tilley. "Addicks an'
Bowden they done the best; Abel an' me we had but a slim fare. We went
out 'arly, but not so 'arly as sometimes; looked like a poor mornin'. I got
nine haddick, all small, and seven fish; the rest on 'em got more fish than
haddick. Well, I don't expect they feel,like bitin' every day; we l'arn to
humor 'em a little, an' let 'em have their way 'bout it. These plaguey
dog-fish kind of worry 'em." Mr. Tilley pronounced the last sentence
with much sympathy, as if he looked upon himself as a true friend of all
the haddock and codfish that lived on the fishing grounds, and so we
parted.

Later in the afternoon I went along the beach again until I came to
the foot of Mr. Tilley's land, and found his rough track across the cobble-
stones and rocks to the field edge, where there was a heavy piece of old
wreck timber, like a ship's bone, full of tree-nails. From this a little
footpath, narrow with one man's treading, led up across the small green
field that made Mr. Tilley's whole estate, except a straggling pasture that
tilted on edge up the steep hillside beyond the house and road. I could
hear the tinkle-tankle of a cow-bell somewhere among the spruces by
which the pasture was being walked over and forested from every side; it
was likely to be called the wood lot before long, but the field was
unmolested. I could not see a bush or a brier anywhere within its walls,
and hardly a stray pebble showed itself. This was most surprising in that
country of firm ledges, and scattered stones which all the walls that
industry could devise had hardly begun to clear away off the land. In the
narrow field I noticed some stout stakes, apparently planted at random
in the grass and among the hills of potatoes, but carefully painted yellow
and white to match the house, a neat sharp-edged little dwelling, which

looked strangely modern for its owner. I should have much sooner believed that the smart young wholesale egg merchant of the Landing was its occupant than Mr. Tilley, since a man's house is really but his larger body, and expresses in a way his nature and character.

I went up the field, following the smooth little path to the side door. As for using the front door, that was a matter of great ceremony; the long grass grew close against the high stone step, and a snowberry bush leaned over it, top-heavy with the weight of a morning-glory vine that had managed to take what the fishermen might call a half hitch about the door-knob. Elijah Tilley came to the side door to receive me; he was knitting a blue yarn stocking without looking on, and was warmly dressed for the season in a thick blue flannel shirt with white crockery buttons, a faded waistcoat and trousers heavily patched at the knees. These were not his fishing clothes. There was something delightful in the grasp of his hand, warm and clean, as if it never touched anything but the comfortable woolen yarn, instead of cold sea water and slippery fish.

"What are the painted stakes for, down in the field?" I hastened to ask, and he came out a step or two along the path to see; and looked at the stakes as if his attention were called to them for the first time.

"Folks laughed at me when I first bought this place an' come here to live," he explained. "They said 'twa'n't no kind of a field privilege at all; no place to raise anything, all full o' stones. I was aware 'twas good land, an' I worked some on it — odd times when I didn't have nothin' else on hand — till I cleared them loose stones all out. You never see a prettier piece than 'tis now; now did ye? Well, as for them painted marks, them's my buoys. I struck on to some heavy rocks that didn't show none, but a plow'd be liable to ground on 'em, an' so I ketched holt an' buoyed 'em same's you see. They don't trouble me no more'n if they wa'n't there."

"You haven't been to sea for nothing," I said laughing.

"One trade helps another," said Elijah with an amiable smile. "Come right in an' set down. Come in an' rest ye," he exclaimed, and led the way into his comfortable kitchen. The sunshine poured in at the two further windows, and a cat was curled up sound asleep on the table that stood between them. There was a new-looking light oilcloth of a tiled pattern on the floor, and a crockery teapot, large for a household of only one person, stood on the bright stove. I ventured to say that somebody must be a very good housekeeper.

"That's me," acknowledged the old fisherman with frankness. "There ain't nobody here but me. I try to keep things looking right, same's poor dear left 'em. You set down here in this chair, then you can look off an' see the water. None on 'em thought I was goin' to get along alone, no way, but I wa'n't goin' to have my house turned upsi' down an' all changed about; no, not to please nobody. I was the only one knew just how she liked to have things set, poor dear, an' I said I was goin' to make shift, and I have made shift. I'd rather tough it out alone." And he sighed heavily, as if to sigh were his familiar consolation.

We were both silent for a minute; the old man looked out the window, as if he had forgotten I was there.

"You must miss her very much?" I said at last.

"I do miss her," he answered, and sighed again. "Folks all kep' repeatin' that time would ease me, but I can't find it does. No, I miss her just the same every day."

"How long is it since she died?" I asked.

"Eight year now, come the first of October. It don't seem near so long. I've got a sister that comes and stops 'long o' me a little spell, spring an' fall, an' odd times if I send after her. I ain't near so good a hand to sew as I be to knit, and she's very quick to set everything to rights. She's a married woman with a family; her son's folks lives at home, an' I can't make no great claim on her time. But it makes me a kind o' good excuse, when I do send, to help her a little; she ain't none too well off. Poor dear always liked her, and we used to contrive our ways together. 'Tis full as easy to be alone. I set here an' think it all over, an' think considerable when the weather's bad to go outside. I get so some days it feels as if poor dear might step right back into this kitchen. I keep a-watchin' them doors as if she might step in to ary one. Yes, ma'am, I keep a-lookin' off an' droppin' o' my stitches; that's just how it seems. I can't git over losin' of her no way nor no how. Yes, ma'am, that's just how it seems to me."

I did not say anything, and he did not look up.

"I git feelin' so sometimes I have to lay everything by an' go out door. She was a sweet pretty creatur' long's she lived," the old man added mournfully. "There's that little rockin' chair o' her'n, I set an' notice it an' think how strange 'tis a creatur' like her should be gone an' that chair be here right in its old place."

"I wish I had known her; Mrs. Todd told me about your wife one day," I said.

"You'd have liked to come and see her; all the folks did," said poor Elijah. "She'd been so pleased to hear everything and see somebody new that took such an int'rest. She had a kind o' gift to make it pleasant for folks. I guess likely Almiry Todd told you she was a pretty woman, especially in her young days; late years, too, she kep' her looks and come to be so pleasant lookin'. There, 't ain't so much matter, I shall be done afore a great while. No; I sha'n't trouble the fish a great sight more."

The old widower sat with his head bowed over his knitting, as if he were hastily shortening the very thread of time. The minutes went slowly by. He stopped his work and clasped his hands firmly together. I saw he had forgotten his guest, and I kept the afternoon watch with him. At last he looked up as if but a moment had passed of his continual loneliness.

"Yes, ma'am, I'm one that has seen trouble," he said, and began to knit again.

The visible tribute of his careful housekeeping, and the clean bright room which had once enshrined his wife, and now enshrined her memory, was very moving to me; he had no thought for any one else or for any other place. I began to see her myself in her home, — a delicate-looking, faded little woman, who leaned upon his rough strength and affectionate heart, who was always watching for his boat out of this very window, and who always opened the door and welcomed him when he came home.

"I used to laugh at her, poor dear," said Elijah, as if he read my thought. "I used to make light of her timid notions. She used to be fearful when I was out in bad weather or baffled about gittin' ashore. She used to say the time seemed long to her, but I've found out all about it now. I used to be dreadful thoughtless when I was a young man and the fish was bitin' well. I'd stay out late some o' them days, an' I expect she'd watch an' watch an' lose heart a-waitin'. My heart alive! what a supper she'd git, an' be right there watchin' from the door, with somethin' over her head if 'twas cold, waitin' to hear all about it as I come up the field. Lord, how I think o' all them little things!"

"This was what she called the best room; in this way," he said presently, laying his knitting on the table, and leading the way across the front entry and unlocking a door, which he threw open with an air of pride. The best room seemed to me a much sadder and more empty place than the kitchen; its conventionalities lacked the simple perfection of the humbler room and failed on the side of poor ambition; it was only when one remembered what patient saving, and what high respect for society in the abstract go to such furnishing that the little parlor was interesting at all. I could imagine the great day of certain purchases, the bewildering shops of the next large town, the aspiring anxious woman, the clumsy sea-tanned man in his best clothes, so eager to be pleased, but at ease only when they were safe back in the sailboat again, going down the bay with their precious freight, the hoarded money all spent and nothing to think of but tiller and sail. I looked at the unworn carpet, the glass vases on the mantelpiece with their prim bunches of bleached swamp grass and dusty marsh rosemary, and I could read the history of Mrs. Tilley's best room from its very beginning.

"You see for yourself what beautiful rugs she could make; now I'm going to show you her best tea things she thought so much of," said the master of the house, opening the door of a shallow cupboard. "That's real chiny, all of it on those two shelves," he told me proudly. "I bought it all myself, when we was first married, in the port of Bordeaux. There never was one single piece of it broke until — Well, I used to say, long as she lived, there never was a piece broke, but long at the last I noticed she'd look kind o' distressed, an' I thought 'twas 'count o' me boastin'. When they asked if they should use it when the folks was here to supper, time o' her funeral, I knew she'd want to have everything nice, and I said 'certain.' Some o' the women they come runnin' to me an' called me, while they was takin' of the chiny down, an' showed me there was one o' the cups broke an' the pieces wropped in paper and pushed way back here, corner o' the shelf. They didn't want me to go an' think they done it. Poor dear! I had to put right out o' the house when I see that. I knowed in one minute how 'twas. We'd got so used to sayin' 'twas all there just's I fetched it home, an' so when she broke that cup somehow or 'nother she couldn't frame no words to come an 'tell me. She couldn't think 'twould vex me, 'twas her own hurt pride. I guess there wa'n't no other secret ever lay between us."

The French cups with their gay sprigs of pink and blue, the best tumblers, an old flowered bowl and tea caddy, and a japanned waiter or two adorned the shelves. These, with a few daguerreotypes in a little square pile, had the closet to themselves, and I was conscious of much pleasure in seeing them. One is shown over many a house in these days where the interest may be more complex, but not more definite.

"Those were her best things, poor dear," said Elijah as he locked the door again. "She told me that last summer before she was taken away that she couldn't think o' anything more she wanted, there was everything in the house, an' all her rooms was furnished pretty. I was goin' over to the Port, an' inquired for errands. I used to ask her to say what she wanted, cost or no cost — she was a very reasonable woman, an' 'twas the place where she done all but her extra shopping. It kind o' chilled me up when she spoke so satisfied."

"You don't go out fishing after Christmas?" I asked, as we came back to the bright kitchen.

"No; I take stiddy to my knitting after January sets in," said the old seafarer. " 'Tain't worth while, fish make off into deeper water an' you can't stand no such perishin' for the sake o' what you get. I leave out a few traps in sheltered coves an' do a little lobsterin' on fair days. The young fellows braves it out, some on 'em; but, for me, I lay in my winter's yarn an' set here where 'tis warm, an' knit an' take my comfort. Mother learnt me once when I was a lad; she was a beautiful knitter herself. I was laid up with a bad knee, an' she said 'twould take up my time an' help her; we was a large family. They'll buy all the folks can do down here to Addicks' store. They say our Dunnet stockin's is gettin' to be celebrated up to Boston, — good quality o' wool an' even knittin' or somethin'. I've always been called a pretty hand to do nettin', but seines is master cheap to what they used to be when they was all hand worked. I change off to nettin' long towards spring, and I piece up my trawls and lines and get my fishin' stuff to rights. Lobster pots they require attention, but I make 'em up in spring weather when it's warm there in the barn. No; I ain't one o' them that likes to set an' do nothin'."

"You see the rugs, poor dear did them; she wa'n't very partial to knittin'," old Elijah went on, after he had counted his stitches. "Our rugs is beginnin' to show wear, but I can't master none o' them womanish tricks. My sister, she tinkers 'em up. She said last time she was here that she guessed they'd last my time."

"The old ones are always the prettiest," I said.

"You ain't referrin' to the braided ones now?" answered Mr. Tilley. "You see ours is braided for the most part, an' their good looks is all in the beginnin'. Poor dear used to say they made an easier floor. I go shufflin' round the house same's if 'twas a bo't, and I always used to be stubbin' up the corners o' the hooked kind. Her an' me was always havin' our jokes together same's a boy an' girl. Outsiders never'd know nothin' about it to see us. She had nice manners with all, but to me there was nobody so entertainin'. She'd take off anybody's natural talk winter evenin's when we set here alone, so you'd think 'twas them a-speakin'. There, there!"

I saw that he had dropped a stitch again, and was snarling the blue yarn round his clumsy fingers. He handled it and threw it off at arm's length as if it were a cod line; and frowned impatiently, but I saw a tear shining on his cheek.

I said that I must be going, it was growing late, and asked if I might come again, and if he would take me out to the fishing grounds someday.

"Yes, come any time you want to," said my host, " 'tain't so pleasant as when poor dear was here. Oh, I didn't want to lose her an' she didn't want to go, but it had to be. Such things ain't for us to say; there's no yes an' no to it."

"You find Almiry Todd one o' the best o' women?" said Mr. Tilley as we parted. He was standing in the doorway and I had started off down the narrow green field. "No, there ain't a better hearted woman in the State o' Maine. I've known her from a girl. She's had the best o' mothers. You tell her I'm liable to fetch her up a couple or three nice good mackerel early tomorrow," he said. "Now don't let it slip your mind. Poor dear, she always thought a sight o' Almiry, and she used to remind me there was nobody to fish for her; but I don't rec'lect it as I ought to. I see you drop a line yourself very handy now an' then."

We laughed together like the best of friends, and I spoke again about the fishing grounds, and confessed that I had no fancy for a southerly breeze and a ground swell.

"Nor me neither," said the old fisherman. "Nobody likes 'em, say what they may. Poor dear was disobliged by the mere sight of a bo't. Almiry's got the best o' mothers, I expect you know; Mis' Blackett out to Green Island; and we was always plannin' to go out when summer come; but there, I couldn't pick no day's weather that seemed to suit her just right. I never set out to worry her neither, 'twa'n't no kind o' use; she was so pleasant we couldn't have no fret nor trouble. 'Twas never 'you dear an' you darlin' ' afore folks, an' 'you divil' behind the door!"

As I looked back from the lower end of the field I saw him still standing, a lonely figure in the doorway. "Poor dear," I repeated to myself half aloud; "I wonder where she is and what she knows of the little world she left. I wonder what she has been doing these eight years!"

I gave the message about the mackerel to Mrs. Todd.

"Been visitin' with 'Lijah?" she asked with interest. "I expect you had kind of a dull session; he ain't the talkin' kind; dwellin' so much long o' fish seems to make 'em lose the gift o' speech." But when I told her that Mr. Tilley had been talking to me that day, she interrupted me quickly.

"Then 'twas all about his wife, an' he can't say nothin' too pleasant neither. She was modest with strangers, but there ain't one o' her old friends can ever make up her loss. For me, I don't want to go there no more. There's some folks you miss and some folks you don't, when they're gone, but there ain't hardly a day I don't think o' dear Sarah Tilley. She was always right there; yes, you knew just where to find her like a plain flower. 'Lijah's worthy enough; I do esteem 'Lijah, but he's a ploddin' man."

XXI

The Backward View

AT LAST IT WAS the time of late summer, when the house was cool and damp in the morning, and all the light seemed to come through green leaves; but at the first step out of doors the sunshine always laid a warm hand on my shoulder, and the clear, high sky seemed to lift quickly as I looked at it. There was no autumnal mist on the coast, nor any August fog; instead of these, the sea, the sky, all the long shore line and the inland hills, with every bush of bay and every fir-top, gained a deeper color and a sharper clearness. There was something shining in the air, and a kind of lustre on the water and the pasture grass, — a northern look that, except at this moment of the year, one must go far to seek. The sunshine of a northern summer was coming to its lovely end.

The days were few then at Dunnet Landing, and I let each of them slip away unwillingly as a miser spends his coins. I wished to have one of my first weeks back again, with those long hours when nothing happened except the growth of herbs and the course of the sun. Once I had not even known where to go for a walk; now there were many delightful things to be done and done again, as if I were in London. I felt hurried and full of pleasant engagements, and the days flew by like a handful of flowers flung to the sea wind.

At last I had to say good-by to all my Dunnet Landing friends, and my homelike place in the little house, and return to the world in which I feared to find myself a foreigner. There may be restrictions to such a summer's happiness, but the ease that belongs to simplicity is charming enough to make up for whatever a simple life may lack, and the gifts of peace are not for those who live in the thick of battle.

I was to take the small unpunctual steamer that went down the bay in the afternoon, and I sat for a while by my window looking out on the green herb garden, with regret for company. Mrs. Todd had hardly spoken all day except in the briefest and most disapproving way; it was as if we were on the edge of a quarrel. It seemed impossible to take my departure with anything like composure. At last I heard a footstep, and looked up to find that Mrs. Todd was standing at the door.

"I've seen to everything now," she told me in an unusually loud and business-like voice. "Your trunks are on the w'arf by this time. Cap'n

Bowden he come and took 'em down himself, an' is going to see that they're safe aboard. Yes, I've seen to all your 'rangements," she repeated in a gentler tone. "These things I've left on the kitchen table you'll want to carry by hand; the basket needn't be returned. I guess I shall walk over towards the Port now an' inquire how old Mis' Edward Caplin is."

I glanced at my friend's face, and saw a look that touched me to the heart. I had been sorry enough before to go away.

"I guess you'll excuse me if I ain't down there to stand around on the w'arf and see you go," she said, still trying to be gruff. "Yes, I ought to go over and inquire for Mis' Edward Caplin; it's her third shock, and if mother gets in on Sunday she'll want to know just how the old lady is." With this last word Mrs. Todd turned and left me as if with sudden thought of something she had forgotten, so that I felt sure she was coming back, but presently I heard her go out of the kitchen door and walk down the path toward the gate. I could not part so; I ran after her to say good-by, but she shook her head and waved her hand without looking back when she heard my hurrying steps, and so went away down the street.

When I went in again the little house had suddenly grown lonely, and my room looked empty as it had the day I came. I and all my belongings had died out of it, and I knew how it would seem when Mrs. Todd came back and found her lodger gone. So we die before our own eyes; so we see some chapters of our lives come to their natural end.

I found the little packages on the kitchen table. There was a quaint West Indian basket which I knew its owner had valued, and which I had once admired; there was an affecting provision laid beside it for my seafaring supper, with a neatly tied bunch of southernwood and a twig of bay, and a little old leather box which held the coral pin that Nathan Todd brought home to give to poor Joanna.

There was still an hour to wait, and I went up to the hill just above the schoolhouse and sat there thinking of things, and looking off to sea, and watching for the boat to come in sight. I could see Green Island, small and darkly wooded at that distance; below me were the houses of the village with their apple-trees and bits of garden ground. Presently, as I looked at the pastures beyond, I caught a last glimpse of Mrs. Todd herself, walking slowly in the footpath that led along, following the shore toward the Port. At such a distance one can feel the large, positive qualities that control a character. Close at hand, Mrs. Todd seemed able and warm-hearted and quite absorbed in her bustling industries, but her distant figure looked mateless and appealing, with something about it that was strangely self-possessed and mysterious. Now and then she stooped to pick something, — it might have been her favorite pennyroyal, — and at last I lost sight of her as she slowly crossed an open space on one of the higher points of land, and disappeared again behind a dark clump of juniper and the pointed firs.

As I came away on the little coastwise steamer, there was an old sea running which made the surf leap high on all the rocky shores. I stood on deck, looking back, and watched the busy gulls agree and turn, and sway together down the long slopes of air, then separate hastily and plunge into the waves. The tide was setting in, and plenty of small fish were coming with it, unconscious of the silver flashing of the great birds overhead and the quickness of their fierce beaks. The sea was full of life and spirit, the tops of the waves flew back as if they were winged like the gulls themselves, and like them had the freedom of the wind. Out in the main channel we passed a bent-shouldered old fisherman bound for the evening round among his lobster traps. He was toiling along with short oars, and the dory tossed and sank and tossed again with the steamer's waves. I saw that it was old Elijah Tilley, and though we had so long been strangers we had come to be warm friends, and I wished that he had waited for one of his mates, it was such hard work to row along shore through rough seas and tend the traps alone. As we passed I waved my hand and tried to call to him, and he looked up and answered my farewells by a solemn nod. The little town, with the tall masts of its disabled schooners in the inner bay, stood high above the flat sea for a few minutes then it sank back into the uniformity of the coast, and became indistinguishable from the other towns that looked as if they were crumbled on the furzy-green stoniness of the shore.

The small outer islands of the bay were covered among the ledges with turf that looked as fresh as the early grass; there had been some days of rain the week before, and the darker green of the sweet-fern was scattered on all the pasture heights. It looked like the beginning of summer ashore, though the sheep, round and warm in their winter wool, betrayed the season of the year as they went feeding along the slopes in the low afternoon sunshine. Presently the wind began to blow, and we struck out seaward to double the long sheltering headland of the cape, and when I looked back again, the islands and the headland had run together and Dunnet Landing and all its coasts were lost to sight.